KU-530-985

Cathy Gillen Thacker

A TEXAS CHRISTMAS

™ MILLS & BOON®

Pure reading pleasure

All the characters in this book have no existence outside
the imagination of the author, and have no relation
whatsoever to anyone bearing the same name or names.
They are not even distantly inspired by any individual
known or unknown to the author, and all the incidents
are pure invention.

All Rights Reserved including the right of reproduction
in whole or in part in any form. This edition is published
by arrangement with Harlequin Enterprises II BV/S.à.r.l.
The text of this publication or any part thereof may
not be reproduced or transmitted in any form or
by any means, electronic or mechanical, including
photocopying, recording, storage in an information
retrieval system, or otherwise, without the written
permission of the publisher.

® and TM are trademarks owned and used by the
trademark owner and/or its licensee. Trademarks marked
with ® are registered with the United Kingdom Patent
Office and/or the Office for Harmonisation in the
Internal Market and in other countries.

First published in Great Britain 2007
Large Print edition 2007
Silhouette Books Limited, Eton House,
18-24 Paradise Road, Richmond, Surrey, TW9 1SR

© Cathy Gillen Thacker 2006

ISBN: 978 0 263 19885 0

Set in Times Roman 16¼ on 19 pt.
35-1207-65552

Printed and bound in Great Britain
by Antony Rowe Ltd, Chippenham, Wiltshire

20178077

MORAY COUNCIL
LIBRARIES &
INFORMATION SERVICES

F

CATHY GILLEN THACKER

married her high school sweetheart and hasn't had a dull moment since. Why? you ask. Well, there were three kids, various pets, any number of automobiles, several moves across the country, his and hers careers and sundry other experiences (some of which were exciting and some of which weren't). But mostly, there was love and friendship and laughter, and lots of experiences she wouldn't trade for the world.

For my buddy Regan, the
best canine companion this writer
could ever have. And definitely my
best Christmas present ever.

Chapter One

Kevin McCabe knew thirteen-and-one-half days of pure unadulterated bliss were too good to be true. It figured that on his way back to Laramie, Texas, he would see something that just had to be investigated. And that the unmarked white van currently backed up to the rear door of the Blackberry Hill mansion would be in an area with no cell phone connections. Had he been driving his work vehicle he'd have had a way to communicate his concern. Instead, he was driving the battered four-wheel drive Jeep he'd owned since high school. It had no two-way radio or emergency communication system.

After pulling over to the side of the winding rural road and watching a woman carry armloads of stuff out of the house, stash it in the van, then dart back into the residence via the side door, he decided to scope out the situation himself. If it had been just material possessions in question, Kevin would have waited for backup. But an eighty-five-year-old woman owned the property. And Miss Sadie had had a bad year already, losing her husband of sixty-two years. Kevin wasn't sure if she was back yet from that six-week recuperative cruise she had been on, but he knew, as did everyone else in the close-knit community, that she was due home any day. Chances were, she wasn't there now, hadn't walked in to witness the theft, or worse, been there when the thieves arrived. But if she *was* there, Kevin couldn't drive off and leave her. Not without first making sure Miss Sadie was okay.

Keeping an eye out for anything else suspicious, he drove slowly toward the pink brick Georgian house with the weathered gray shutters, stopping just short of the white van. Wishing he had a way to check the license plates, he cut the engine and got out. He walked down the long, tree-lined driveway toward the open side door, then paused to look in the windows of the rented van. It was loaded with Miss Sadie's valuables, all right, he noted grimly. Everything from a Tiffany lamp to her jewelry box and favorite rocking chair.

"May I help you?" a feminine voice asked coolly from the top of the steps. Christmas music floated merrily from the interior of the house.

Time to appear clueless about what was going on. Kevin turned away from the loot with his best "Aw, shucks, ma'am, I'm just a dumb country boy" grin, and immediately noticed several things about the woman standing beneath the portico. She wasn't a local. He was sure of that because had he ever encountered this very beautiful woman, even in passing, he definitely would have remembered her. She was dressed in a pair of olive wool slacks that lovingly gloved her slender hips and long lissome legs. A white cotton shirt, open at the throat, lay beneath an argyle sweater vest and tweed blazer. Her accent said Texas, born and bred. Her boots were the high-heeled, soft-leather type city slickers wore, their only purpose to change the tilt of her posture and make her legs look damn good. Which they did.

Reminding himself he would need to make a positive ID later, Kevin estimated the interloper was around five foot six, one hundred and twenty pounds, close to his own twenty-seven years in age and, as previously noted, curvy in all the right places. Her copper hair fell to her chin in a riot of springy curls he found incredibly sexy. And his attraction to the perpetrator didn't end there. She had an angelically round face with a straight, slender nose and a thin upper lip countered by a full lush lower lip, just right for kissing. Her peachy skin was fair and flawless save for the sprinkling of freckles; her savvy blue eyes were intelligent, wide-set and long-lashed.

Not surprisingly, she was incredibly nervous—and pretending not to be, even as she stood there with a five-foot-high plastic candy cane beside her, cupped loosely in her right hand. Although he couldn't fathom what she was doing with that ridiculous thing. The faded red-and-white plastic lawn ornament didn't look like something *anyone* would want to steal.

Reminding himself she could be a lot more dangerous than her sweet and sexy appearance indicated, he paused at the bottom of the stairs. Tipping his hat in her direction, he acted every bit as oblivious to the criminal wrongdoing going on as the situation demanded. "Hello. I'm Kevin McCabe."

THAT WAS THE PROBLEM with agreeing to do a last-minute job like this, in an unfamiliar part of the state, Noelle Kringle noted, not buying the name he had given her for one instant. She didn't need this kind of trouble two weeks before Christmas. And the six-foot-tall hunk in front of her was heartache personified.

Or at least he would have been if he'd bothered to clean up. The golden-brown hair peeking from beneath the brim of a bone-colored Stetson hat and falling haphazardly across his brows, over his ears and down the nape of his neck needed to be combed and cut. She estimated it had been weeks since his boyishly handsome face had been shaved. And that, she couldn't help but note a little wistfully, was a shame. The scraggly, dark brown whiskers on his face detracted from his nicely chiseled features and the sexy cleft in his chin. Not that she needed to be admiring the sensual lips, square masculine chin and arresting brown eyes of a man in ripped jeans, and a grime-smeared flannel shirt and gray Henley that had both seen better days. Especially when she feared she knew exactly why he was surreptitiously scoping out everything about the place—and her. He'd heard the rumors, too.

He moved closer, drawing her attention to the implicit threat in his broad shoulders and street-fighter's build. This was not a man she'd want to meet in a dark alley. This was a man she would want on her side. Although for whatever reason, despite his outwardly laid-back manner, he did not seem to be. "I stopped by to see Miss Sadie, if she's available," he began, casually enough.

After the way she had been raised, Noelle could spot a pretender a mile away. Not that he needed to know she was onto his game. "Actually, she's not,"

Noelle replied with another cool smile, urging him to hurry on back to wherever he had come from.

He kept his eyes on hers. "Do you know when she'll be back?"

"No." Noelle chanced a look behind her toward the interior of the house and, to her immense relief, heard nothing but the strains of "Oh Come All Ye Faithful." "I don't."

"I see." He propped one boot on the bottom step. Leaning forward, he rested an elbow on his thigh. Settling in for the duration, he charmed her with a smile. "And you are…?"

Noelle ignored the shiver of awareness that sifted through her. There was no way she was giving out that information in this day and age. She glanced at the wintry gray sky, wishing for a burst of rain that would send him running. "Too busy to stand here chatting with you." She finished his sentence for him, turning to go back in the house.

He straightened and moved along the outside of the railing. He walked right next to her so she couldn't avoid looking at him, even as he peered past her at the closed draperies and blinds that obscured the windows of every room of the house. He seemed to be tactically assessing the situation even as he formulated his next move. Another very bad sign, she thought as her pulse picked up even more.

"You seem stressed," he stated.

You don't know the half of it.

"Is there a problem in there?"

She listened hard and, to her continued relief, still heard no "suspicious" sounds coming from inside.

He paused, offered another ingratiating look. "Anything I can help you—or Miss Sadie—with?"

Noelle stopped at the edge of the landing and gripped the big plastic candy cane in front of her. "No. And there won't be a problem if you leave now." She made no effort to disguise the warning.

As she had suspected, the sexy stranger did not respond well to the veiled threat. "And if I don't?"

Noelle scanned the drive for the help that should be coming. Any minute now. All she had to do was stall… And if that meant take her bravado to the next level, so be it. She let him squirm for a few minutes. "Then I'll be forced to make a citizen's arrest."

Something shifted in his gaze, and his choked laughter turned into a cough. "On what grounds?" he asked in obvious disbelief.

She held her head high and kept her expression composed. "Coming onto Miss Sadie's property without an invitation and then refusing to leave when asked."

He tipped his hat back, letting her see his insulted expression. "I am not trespassing."

She regarded him dubiously, letting him know that she wasn't stupid, either. "We'll let the sheriff's department decide that. Frankly, I think they're going to be on my side."

The corners of his lips crooked up. "Doubtful, since I work for the sheriff's department."

She tilted her head and gave him the look she reserved for anyone who tried to snow her. "Really."

"Yes."

She scanned him quickly, beginning to enjoy this verbal sparring match. "Then they must have some very peculiar uniforms."

He took off his hat and shoved his hand through clean, rumpled hair. "Obviously, I'm not on duty now."

"If you ever were," Noelle muttered beneath her breath, wondering why coming outside to let this potential felon know the house was indeed occupied and thereby not available for any yuletide plundering had ever seemed like a good idea. She should have just stayed inside and hoped he didn't do anything crazy—like break a window or jimmy a door lock—while she waited for help to arrive. Instead, she was out here, with only a plastic candy cane to protect her, chatting with a smooth-talking hottie whose self-confidence apparently knew no bounds.

"Hey—" he angled a thumb at his chest, looking harmless enough for the moment "—no need to insult me."

Noelle refused to let down her guard. Still trying to buy time and keep him from figuring out she was not alone, she bantered right back, "You started it."

His brows knit together. "How?"

Telling herself she was definitely not enjoying

their repartee, Noelle gave him a look that let him know she was not impressed. "By insulting my intelligence."

Frowning, he waited for her to go on.

Noelle studied his hands, wondering how his body could be so clean when his clothes were so impossibly grungy. "Pretending to be a McCabe, for starters."

"What makes you think I'm not?" he asked.

Because, as she had learned very early in life, the first rule of thumb when it came to running a con was to gain trust—and entrée—to your mark, find common ground and get close any way you could. A swift way to do that was by selecting a respected last name and claiming a familial connection. Rule number two—most people never doubted the name you gave upon introduction. It simply didn't occur to them to question it. When a con met a mark who did, he or she usually just saved themselves the trouble and moved on. "The McCabes are one of the most well-respected families in the state." Noelle gave a phony smile. "They don't have a slacker among them."

His spine stiffened. "I assure you I am quite hardworking and successful."

"Not to mention a member of law enforcement."

The scowl on his face deepened. "I am a deputy with the Laramie County Sheriff's Department."

She nodded in exaggerated agreement, aware he hadn't so much as flashed a badge. Another telltale sign. "Sure you are. They always employ unkempt and unshaven—" although not unwashed "—bums in filthy clothing."

He looked as if he didn't know whether to laugh or strike back. "So now I'm a trespassing bum?" He rubbed his jaw with the flat of his hand in a parody of thoughtfulness. "Is that a technical term?" He tilted his head. "Maybe you should call that in and let them know you've got a vagrant on your hands. And while you're at it, that the bum's name is Kevin McCabe."

Noelle tapped her foot on the landing and felt the rotting wood shift uncertainly beneath her feet. "No need," she announced, "since they'll be here at any minute."

He swept off his hat and started up the first two

steps. They creaked beneath his weight, shedding splinters of wood and aging paint. "Look, you can dis me personally all you want, later. Right now I want to check on Miss Sadie."

"I told you she's not here," Noelle said impatiently, wondering whose idea it was to put wood steps where they would be exposed to the rain, and then fail to keep them waterproofed and painted.

"Well, guess what?" The wood creaked again as he climbed yet another step. "I don't believe you."

"Then you're wrong." Noelle took one step down.

"In fact—" he came up one more "—I think you're hiding something."

Only the most important thing in the world to me. Only the reason I took this opportunity so close to the holidays—against my better judgment. Only the reason I'm now so very sorry that I did.

He lounged against the railing, studying her openly. "And I'm not leaving until I find out what you're trying to keep me from discovering."

Panic swept through her. Noelle went down

another step, the candy cane held in front of her like a battering ram. "I don't care who you are or what you think. There is no way you are getting past me into this house," she told him.

He abruptly became reasonable again. "Look, I just want to make sure Miss Sadie and her property are all right."

Part of Noelle—the part that had already looked deep into his eyes and found them to be inherently kind—wanted to believe that. The cynical side of her that had learned not to trust anyone, said otherwise. "If you were really with the sheriff's department," she reminded him, "you would already know the answer to that."

He went completely still. For a split second, Noelle could have sworn that was genuine alarm in his eyes. "*Has* something happened to her?" he asked, concerned.

Either he truly cared about Miss Sadie or he was one hell of an actor. Noelle regarded him skeptically. "Everyone around here knows what occurred here the day before yesterday. *I* know, and I don't even live in the area!"

He frowned. "I've been out of touch for the past two weeks. I'm on my way home from a fishing trip."

That might have rung true, in summer. Not December. Although it did explain the clothes.... Resolved not to accept anything he told her without due scrutiny, she lifted a brow. "Fishing for what?"

"Speckled trout, red drum and white bass. I've got my catch on ice in my Jeep if you want to see it."

Okay, that had the ring of truth. However, that didn't mean it was a good idea to let him any closer, especially given whom she had hidden inside Miss Sadie's house. Darn it all. Where was that patrol car? She fixed him with her most threatening glare. "Once again, you need to leave."

His mouth twitched with suppressed amusement. "Or what?"

Obviously he was not used to being ordered around.

"I'll be forced to use this." She waved her

"weapon" threateningly in his direction. "To defend myself."

"Well—" he lifted both hands in a mock display of surrender "—*now* I'm scared."

"You should be," she lied, gripping the large plastic ornament more tightly.

"Oh, I can see you're armed and dangerous." He started toward her once again, wicked speculation gleaming in his eyes.

She backed up ever so slightly, aware the rest of her was suddenly shaking as much as her knees. "I know how to use this."

"What are you going to do with it?" he taunted. "Decorate me?"

"You wish. Now get back!" She lunged toward him.

Probably figuring she was going to aim for his head, he brought his hands up to shield his face. She faked him out and swung low instead. He jumped left, swearing as the candy cane whacked his thigh with a dull thud.

"Hey! Watch what you're doing with that thing!"

Okay, maybe she hadn't actually hurt him,

but she had annoyed him. And now that she had the upper hand... "Now do you take me seriously?" she asked.

He grimaced, eyeing the candy cane, yet still refused to back down the steps. "Ma'am," he drawled, tipping the brim of his hat, "I have from the first."

"Stop calling me 'ma'am'." She prodded at him like a cowpoke herding cattle into a pen.

He gave her a pitying look, then retreated down the steps.

It was a conciliatory move, one she'd be a fool to trust.

"What would you like me to call you?"

Figuring she was going to have to go through with the citizen's arrest after all, since it was taking the sheriff's department so darn long, Noelle followed him down the steep, rickety steps toward the van. Using the candy cane, she motioned for him to keep moving back, until his spine grazed the side of the vehicle. Summoning up every police procedural she had ever seen, Noelle barked, "Get down on your knees."

His brows lifted. "Now, that's a thought."

"And put your hands behind your head," she commanded.

"Even more interesting." He gave her a look that made her flush. "But no."

Ah, heck. Now what? Trying not to think what a ludicrous situation this was, Noelle brandished her "weapon." "Don't make me hurt you—"

"Momma!" a familiar, high-pitched voice cried.

Noelle turned in time to see her two-year-old son stumbling out of the house, carrying a book that was half as big as he was. Noelle jerked in a terrified breath. This was exactly what she had been trying to prevent. "Mikey—!"

"Momma!" Still smiling, her son raced awkwardly across the landing, his feet getting tangled as he reached the top of the stairs.

Aware it would take both hands to catch the twenty-eight-pound toddler, Noelle leaped toward him. "Mikey, no—!"

Too late. He was already pitching forward, tumbling head over heels. Desperate to protect him, Noelle took another leap, cast the candy cane aside and bounded up the stairs in a single vault. She caught her son in her arms midtumble, just as her full weight landed hard on the rickety wooden steps. There was a crunching sound and a sick, scared feeling in her gut as wood splintered beneath them and then gave way. Noelle was sure she was going to break a limb, even as she tried her best to cradle her son protectively to her chest.

And then it was the interloper's turn to save the day. He caught both her and her son in his arms before they could sink all the way through the wood, and pulled them to safety. Wide-eyed, Mikey let out a startled sound that was half cry, half laugh.

"Mikey!" Noelle murmured again, this time shuddering in relief.

Her little boy beamed up at her before reaching over, gently patting Kevin's beard and staring hard into his brown eyes. "Santa?" he asked.

Chapter Two

"He's not Santa, honey."

"Beard," the cute little boy with the copper curls and same vibrant blue eyes as his mother said.

"Yes, he has a beard," she confirmed, squirming in Kevin's arms, even as he tried to help her back on her feet. Not an easy task, since she was still slightly off balance and had a child in her arms. "But this man is not Santa Claus."

"No kidding," a low male voice agreed. Kevin relaxed at the sight of the uniformed lawman coming around the corner of the house. Rio Vasquez had his hand on his holster, but when he spotted the three of them tangled up on the partially collapsed wooden stairs, he dropped his arm and quickened his steps.

"Thank heaven you're here!" Kevin's would-be jailer said.

Rio gave Kevin an odd look that gave nothing away before turning back to the copper-haired beauty. "You're the woman who called in to report an attempted burglary on Miss Sadie's property?"

"Yes. I'm Noelle Kringle," she stated firmly, agitated color flooding her cheeks as she squirmed out of Kevin's arms.

He told himself he wasn't sorry to let her go, that he hadn't really enjoyed holding her soft warm body next to his, any more than he had enjoyed inhaling the lavender scent of her perfume.

"I'm glad you're here, Deputy…Vasquez," Noelle said haughtily, reading the name on his badge. "I was trying to make a citizen's arrest."

Kevin had to give his buddy credit—Rio didn't so much as flinch, even at the phony-sounding name. Instead, he merely lifted his brow and waited for "Noelle Kringle" to go on.

"I saw him checking out the stuff in my van," Noelle continued, with an accusing look aimed Kevin's way.

"Which is when you called the sheriff's department and then hung up on the 9-1-1 operator," Rio guessed.

Noelle nodded. "I came out to stop him from taking anything. He wouldn't leave when I asked him to. So I decided to detain him until you arrived."

Rio made a few notes on the pad in front of him while Noelle shifted her son to her other hip. Noting that the little boy was looking at the holiday storybook he had dropped, Kevin leaned forward to retrieve it. After making sure there were no splinters clinging to it, he handed it back to the kid and was rewarded with a beaming smile.

"Not to mention the fact that he scared me half to death sneaking up on the house that way."

"I would hardly call it sneaking. I turned off the road, drove up the lane and got out of my Jeep."

"Only after sitting out on the berm for a good two or three minutes, casing the property."

Kevin shrugged. "Things looked suspicious. I know Miss Sadie's been out of town. I figured I'd come on up here and figure out what was going on."

Noelle turned back to Rio. "He also claimed he was a lawman, if you can believe that!"

Rio played along. "Really."

"Of course he didn't have a badge."

Kevin wasn't sure whether he was more irked or amused. "I didn't take it with me. I usually don't when I go fishing for two weeks. I mean, who am I going to arrest—a recalcitrant bass?"

Rio narrowed his black eyes in typical enough-with-the-monkey-business manner. "What do you have to say for yourself, McCabe?" he asked.

"Well…" Kevin took his time coming to any conclusions. "I was pretty scared." He pointed at the discarded "weapon." "She was threatening me with that plastic candy cane over there."

Unable to help himself, Rio grinned, then began to chuckle.

Realization flooded Noelle. She did not look pleased by her conclusion, Kevin noted.

"You two know each other?" she asked.

Rio nodded slowly. "Kevin is a deputy with the Laramie County Sheriff's Department, too.

Although you'd never know it by looking at him now."

Some of the color left Noelle's face. She blinked at Kevin in astonishment. "So you *were* telling the truth!"

She didn't need to look quite so amazed. "Ah—yeah." Kevin looked at Rio. "Can you believe it? She didn't think I was a McCabe, either."

Rio swept off his hat and ran his fingers through his black hair. A commiserating smirk dominated his handsome features. "Is that right?"

"She said I looked too disreputable to be a member of that clan."

"Well." Rio sighed and set his hat back on his head. "It *is* an upstanding family. You do not look the least bit respectable."

"Right." Kevin turned back to Noelle, whose eyes were alive with emotion as she cuddled her toddler close to her chest. "What was it you called me—a trespassing bum?"

She flushed a becoming pink, while Rio laughed. "In her defense, you do look pretty seedy at the moment," he teased.

Kevin pretended to be irked. "Speak for yourself." He paused, ready to get down to business. "So what's going on with Miss Sadie?"

"Do you mind if we go inside?" Noelle interrupted, shivering. "It's a little chilly for my son."

"Sure."

Because of the state of the side staircase, they had to enter through the front door, which she unlocked with a key. The last time Kevin had been inside the home had been to pay his respects the previous January, after Miss Sadie's husband, Alfred, died. It had been immaculate. Now, it was dusty and bore the faintly stale air of a house that had been unoccupied. More alarming still, the formal living room was covered with ripped envelopes, and papers were scattered across the floor. Half a dozen suitcases stood in the foyer, and it looked as if a pot of tea had splashed against one cream-colored wall. "What the heck happened here?" he said in shock. "Did someone break in while Miss Sadie was on her cruise?"

Noelle and Rio exchanged a glance that left Kevin feeling he was the one on the outside looking in.

"The property was fine when she arrived home from her cruise day before yesterday," Noelle said. "The problem occurred when she made herself a pot of tea, sat down to catch up on her mail and found out she'd been the victim of identity theft. She got so upset she forgot her suitcases were in the hall, and she tripped as she was headed back to the kitchen to make another pot of tea and telephone the authorities."

Rio added grimly, "She broke her leg and had to have surgery yesterday."

"And now she's been moved to the nursing home across the street for the next six to eight weeks," Noelle continued.

"Your brother Riley is her family doctor and is taking care of her," Rio said.

Kevin looked at Noelle. "How did you get involved?"

"I'm good friends with her great-nephew, Dash Nelson, and I've done a lot of work as an event planner for Miss Sadie in Houston."

That made sense. Kevin knew Miss Sadie split her time between her place in the city and her country home in Laramie County, spending equal amounts in each. Sadie Nelson was a noted philanthropist, always masterminding one charity event or another.

"Dash asked me if I would come up and pick up some things to take over to the nursing home for her. Dressing table, favorite rocking chair… things like that. I didn't think her jewelry—much of which is very valuable—should be left out here under the circumstances, so I put that in the van, too. I figured I would give it to Dash for safekeeping when he gets here later this evening, until Miss Sadie is feeling better."

Kevin had a passing acquaintance with the Houston-based attorney. He was a nice guy. Upstanding. Devoted to his aunt Sadie and late uncle Alfred.

Noelle set her squirming son down on the floor. He took his storybook over to the sofa, climbed up on the cushions and began to "read" to himself. The sweetly voiced chatter about Christmas and snow and Santa Claus had them all smiling.

Kevin turned his attention back to Noelle. She

looked even lovelier in the warm light of the home's interior. "Where is Dash?"

Her lower lip curved into a smile. "He's in Houston. He had to be in court today but should be here later this evening. I'm supposed to meet him at the nursing home."

"Laramie Gardens Home for Seniors," Kevin ascertained.

"Right."

The facility was a combination assisted living and nursing home, the best in the area. Sadie would be well taken care of there.

"Anyway…" Noelle took a deep breath that lifted the soft swell of her breasts. "Sorry about the misunderstanding earlier."

He grinned at her feisty tone, liking the warm flush of color that had come into her cheeks as they talked. "It was entertaining, to be sure."

"Only wish I had been here," Rio interjected good-naturedly.

Kevin knew that was true. He was going to be living this one down forever.

"But I need to get going," she said firmly, taking

charge of the situation once again. "If you two would be so kind and help me take these last three items out to the van, I'll lock up. I want to get to town and back before dark."

It had been a long time since Kevin had encountered a woman with such spunk and vitality. However, he wasn't quite sure yet that he could trust her as Miss Sadie and Dash Nelson apparently did. "You're staying here?"

She stooped to pick up some of the mail scattered here and there. "Yes."

Kevin and Rio bent down to help. "For…?" Kevin asked.

Noelle Kringle's eyes locked with his. "However long Miss Sadie needs me."

CHRISTMAS HAD ALWAYS BEEN a holiday that reminded Noelle of everything she didn't have, but she was determined her son was going to have a better life. She hadn't done right by him in the past, choosing to work nonstop through the festive season in order to bring in as much money as possible for them. But this Christmas was going to be different. She had passed on many of the holiday jobs sent her way, and had scheduled time off for herself until after the new year. And she had begun talking to Mikey about what Christmas meant well in advance, explaining everything from mangers to jolly old St. Nick. Noelle knew Mikey didn't quite get it all yet, but by the time the season was over, he would have a much greater understanding of the rebirth and renewal, hope and happiness that the holiday brought. And they would both be better for it.

Her plans hadn't included running into a sheriff's deputy who set her heart racing. She hadn't been attracted to a man since her husband had died, but she was attracted to Kevin McCabe, even if she didn't want to be. She felt the undeniable physical pull every time she looked into his mesmerizing eyes.

Not that anything was going to happen. The last thing she needed was to get involved with anyone in law enforcement. And that went double for someone as inquisitive as Kevin McCabe, Noelle thought, as she got out of the rented van and moved around to extract Mikey from his car seat.

To her delight, the Laramie Gardens Home for Seniors was a bright and cheerful facility. A huge Christmas tree sparkled in the common room off the lobby. The high school choir was squeezed in against one wall, singing carols to residents seated on the comfortable chairs and sofas. Mikey watched, spellbound, as Noelle checked in at the front desk, then started back to Miss Sadie's room with him perched on her hip.

"Well, one would never guess you had surgery yesterday." Noelle smiled as she walked in. The elegant eighty-five-year-old woman—who bore a striking resemblance to Katherine Hepburn, right down to her auburn-tinted hair and lively eyes—was sitting up in bed. She wore a pale blue hospital gown and robe, and her cheeks were a little more pale than usual, but her hair had been brushed and twisted up into its usual stylish knot on top of her head. As always, the kindness that had drawn Noelle in exuded from the woman in waves. In the seven years Noelle had known her, Miss Sadie had become the grandmother she had always wanted but never had. The way Miss

Sadie doted on Mikey, he might as well have been her great-grandson. Noelle wasn't sure how she would have survived in the three years since Michael, Sr., had died if it hadn't been for Miss Sadie's stabilizing presence in her life. And Noelle owed Sadie's nephew, Dash Nelson, a lot, too. The two were the closest thing she and Mikey had to family these days.

Relieved to see the older woman looking so well, she leaned down to give her a hug.

Miss Sadie pointed to the cast that went from midthigh to instep on her left leg. "Can you believe it? All those years skiing and never one broken bone…"

"You're lucky it wasn't more serious."

"So the doctors said. Hello, Mikey darling."

Mikey grinned and waved both hands frantically. "Mah Sadie!" He lurched far enough out of Noelle's arms for Sadie to deliver the traditional kiss on his small cheek.

"I've got all the things you wanted in the van outside," Noelle said.

"Good." Miss Sadie motioned for her to take a

seat. "I'll have Dash carry them in when he gets here. Meantime, let's talk about the party I'm supposed to be throwing in Houston next week."

Noelle put Mikey on the floor. She reached into her carryall for a miniature Santa sleigh and two toy reindeer and handed them to him. He sat down and began playing. "You sure you're up to that?" In the past, Miss Sadie had divided her time equally between Laramie and Houston. But Christmas Eve and Christmas Day she'd always spent at Blackberry Hill, in the neighborhood where she and her late oilman husband had grown up.

"Oh, yes. It's all I've been able to think about all day."

Noelle plucked her notepad from her shoulder bag. "Any chance you can go back for your traditional open house in Houston?" The party was a hugely popular bash. Noelle had been helping Miss Sadie plan and execute the annual black-tie event for the last seven years.

She shook her head. "My doctors want me here where they can keep an eye on me until the cast comes off in six weeks. Although I did get them to agree to let me spend Christmas Eve and Christmas Day at Blackberry Hill, as usual." She sighed. "So you and I have our work cut out for us. First, we're going to need to notify all the guests that the party in my Houston home is canceled. I'd like to donate all the food and flowers to the Texas Children's Home. And see if the brass quintet we had hired to play at the party would be willing to play there also."

"No problem." Noelle wrote rapidly on the pad in front of her. "I think I can get that done tomorrow."

"Second, since I can't get around on my own right now, I'm going to need your help getting ready for Christmas here."

"I can do that, too." Noelle smiled.

"And then…" Sadie's lower lip trembled. She looked as if she was about to cry. "There is the identity theft to be dealt with."

"Not to worry, dear Aunt Sadie," a voice called warmly from the doorway. "Your nephew Dash is already on the case."

Noelle looked up in time to see Dash Nelson

saunter in. As usual, the accomplished attorney was wearing a suit and tie that perfectly suited his trim, athletic frame. Exuding every bit as much kindness as his beloved great-aunt, Dash paused to pat Noelle's shoulder affectionately and ruffle Mikey's hair, then continued on over to the hospital bed where Miss Sadie sat. "I just got off the phone with the sheriff's department," he informed her, bending to kiss her forehead. "They're sending their fraud expert over to talk to you right away."

Unbidden memories sifted through Noelle. Keeping the smile fixed on her face, she pushed them away. Thankfully, this mess wasn't about her. She could help manage it without worrying about ending up in the middle of it. And in the process she could help repay Miss Sadie and Dash for all they had done for her.

Miss Sadie beamed at them both. "What would I do without you two?"

Dash settled on the end of his aunt's bed. "That's not something you need to worry about, since the two of us aren't going anywhere." He reached over and playfully squeezed Noelle's hand. "Right, Noelle?"

She smiled. Was it her imagination or was Dash suddenly acting a little different around her?

She had no chance to dwell on it, as footsteps sounded in the hall outside Miss Sadie's room. A rap on the door frame preceded a very handsome deputy sticking his head in.

Noelle took a calming breath as she and the interloper regarded each other in contemplative silence.

"Why, Kevin McCabe!" Miss Sadie cried in delight.

His dark eyes alive with interest, Kevin sauntered into the room. "Feel up to talking to me?" he asked without missing a beat.

Miss Sadie nodded and made introductions.

Noelle blushed as Kevin McCabe moved closer, his glance roving over her upturned face. "We've met," she murmured, thrown by the lawman's deliberate proximity to her.

"Although I daresay I wasn't nearly this presentable at the time," Kevin teased, scrubbing a hand across his freshly shaved jaw.

He cleaned up well; Noelle grudgingly gave him that. His tan uniform was crisply ironed, his leather boots bore a subtle glow. And he smelled great, too—like soap and woodsy cologne. She tore her eyes from the cleft in his chin that had been obscured by the beard he'd had just an hour or so earlier. He still needed a haircut, but his thick, golden-brown hair had been brushed into order, and looked just as soft, clean and touchable as ever.

"You must be the department expert on fraud," Dash stated, standing to shake his hand.

Kevin nodded, even as Noelle refused to let him intimidate her with his I'm-in-charge-here body language. She had nothing to hide, at least as far as Miss Sadie's case was concerned.

Mikey looked up from his toys, stared at Kevin curiously—as if trying to reconcile the clean-shaven Kevin with the bearded Kevin—then smiled and went back to playing with his Santa sleigh and reindeer. Noelle knew exactly how her son felt. There was the rough-hewn Kevin who had shown up fresh from a fishing trip, seemingly bent on giving her a hard time, and the good guy lawman standing in front of her. She didn't know which version she found more alluring. She only knew being close to him threatened her peace of mind. And that was something she tried very hard to avoid.

She liked dull. Predictable.

Life, she was sure, would never be those things with Kevin McCabe anywhere in the vicinity.

"I specialize in computer fraud and identity theft," he continued, oblivious to the nature of her thoughts. To her relief, he swiftly got down to business. While Kevin and Miss Sadie went over the specifics, Dash carried her belongings in from the van. Noelle worked on hanging up her clothing, setting up her vanity table and toiletries, favorite antique rocking chair and footstool, side table and reading lamp.

One minute Mikey had been playing nicely near the register beneath the windows. The next time Noelle turned around he was standing next to Kevin, running the sleigh and reindeer from the detective's knee along the outside of his thigh and back again. Kevin continued talking with Miss Sadie, completely at ease.

Embarrassed, Noelle went to intervene. "Mikey, honey—"

"It's okay." Kevin lifted a hand. "I'm used to kids. I don't mind."

Noelle could see he truly didn't, which only made him all the more appealing.

Dash walked back in, carrying Miss Sadie's favorite Tiffany lamp. "Where do you want this?"

"Bedside table," his aunt replied.

"I'm going to need copies of those credit card and debit card statements," Kevin said, rising.

"They're all at Blackberry Hill." Miss Sadie looked at Noelle. "Could you make copies of the statements for him on the copier in my office, dear?"

Noelle told herself she was not at all disappointed that her time with Kevin McCabe had once again come to an end. "No problem."

"Meantime, I assume all the companies involved have been notified." Kevin rocked back on his heels.

"I did that while my aunt was in surgery yesterday, using the credit and debit cards in her wallet," Dash confirmed, every bit as serious about protecting his aunt as Kevin was. "We still have to notify the companies who opened fraudulent accounts in her name without her knowledge or permission."

"I can help with that." Kevin handed over the police report for Sadie to sign.

Noelle noted that Sadie was looking tired. Mikey was beginning to get cranky, too. "I better get this little one some supper," she said.

"I'll stay with Aunt Sadie," Dash promised.

By the time Noelle got back to Blackberry Hill, it was dark and Mikey was starving. From the groceries she had brought with her from Houston, she heated up a toddler chicken-and-noodle casserole and a jar of bite-size green beans in the microwave, poured milk into a sippy cup and cut up a banana. She put on some Christmas music and sat with her son while he ate.

Tired as he was, he had no desire to cut short his bath, so it was another forty-five minutes before she had him in his pajamas and tucked into the pack-and-play crib she used when they traveled. Noelle stayed with him until he went to sleep, made sure the baby monitor was set, then headed back downstairs in time to see headlights arcing across the front of the big house.

Figuring it was Dash, she opened the door and saw Kevin McCabe getting out of a patrol car instead.

Chapter Three

"Expecting someone else?" Kevin asked, surprised by how good it felt to see her.

"Certainly not a trespassing bum."

He grinned at her self-effacing tone, glad she had concluded he really was no threat to her or her son. He wasn't used to being regarded with suspicion. He rubbed a hand across his jaw. "I clean up good, huh?"

"Apparently so." The wind whipped up, sending a chill through the front hall. She waited for him to wipe his feet on the mat, then ushered him inside. Her eyes glimmered with a combination of mischief and warm hospitality he found very appealing. "What can I do for you, Detective McCabe?"

Kevin swept off his hat and held it close to his

chest. He reminded himself he was there on business. Not pleasure. "I wanted to go ahead and get copies of all Miss Sadie's theft-related mail. The sooner we get this situation sorted out for her, the better."

Noelle sobered at the mention of the crime. She pointed wordlessly to the coat rack next to the door, and Kevin hung his Stetson there. "Do you think you're going to be able to figure out who did this?" she asked, leading the way to the formal living room.

Kevin tore his gaze from the alluring sway of her hips. "The culprits are smart. But criminals always trip up eventually. And a single mistake is all we need to arrest them."

Noelle stopped in front of three large stacks of mail. She looked over at Kevin with a frown. "I haven't had a chance to go through any of her mail yet."

Kevin had been hoping that would be the case. "That's okay. I can sort it out."

She ran her teeth across her lush lower lip. "Maybe the kitchen table would be better?"

He eyed the antique settee and the small oval coffee table. She was right. No way was that going to be comfortable. "Probably. Thanks."

Noelle helped him pick up the letters and discarded envelopes. She led the way to the kitchen. While he began sorting the mail into piles, she turned on a baby monitor and set it on the corner of the counter. "I was just about to have dinner." She looked in the freezer compartment of the refrigerator and studied a stack of glossy white cardboard boxes, the exact thing he would have been doing had he been home alone tonight. "Can I get you anything?"

Yes. You.

Where the hell had that thought come from?

"I don't want to intrude." Maybe this hadn't been such a good idea.

She waved off his protest. "We have chicken fettuccini and broccoli, beef and broccoli and lemon chicken and broccoli."

Kevin detected a theme. "Got a thing for broccoli, do you?"

Her blue eyes gleamed at his teasing tone. She

tilted her head to one side and regarded him with mock gravity, declaring stubbornly, "I'm not admitting to anything, Detective."

He grinned at her playful attitude. This was a woman who could be a lot of fun. Another reason he needed to watch his step. "You're sure it's no trouble?" he asked casually, doing his best to stay on task.

She shrugged a slender shoulder. "I can heat two dinners in the microwave as easily as one."

"Thanks, then," Kevin said over the rumbling of his stomach. "I'd appreciate it. I haven't had time to grab dinner this evening, either."

She went back to studying the selections. "And your choice is?"

He sorted credit card statements in one pile, what looked to be party invitations and Christmas cards in another. "Whichever broccoli dinner you least want to eat. It doesn't matter. They all sound pretty good."

She took out two and began unwrapping them. "You eat a lot of frozen dinners?"

Kevin made a third pile for junk mail while she

set the microwave timer. "Doesn't every single person who's too lazy to cook on a regular basis?"

She lounged against the counter and folded her arms in front of her. "So you really were fishing."

Trying not to note how delectable she looked in the soft kitchen light, with her mussed hair, flushed cheeks and lively blue eyes, he drawled, "That's right."

She looked him up and down. "By yourself."

"Well…" He warmed at her skeptical tone. "There were a few fishes there. But I can't really call them friends."

Her smile widened. "Especially the ones you caught and plan to eat."

"Exactly."

Their eyes met. Held. Kevin felt another jolt of physical attraction.

Noelle sobered before his thoughts could go from reality to fantasy in three seconds flat. "I feel pretty foolish about what happened earlier," she told him softly.

He pushed away the memory of her body caught against his. So her breasts were soft and full, the rest of her slender and fit. So she smelled like crushed lilacs on a sunny day. That didn't mean he had to desire her, any more than he had to notice the scent of baby powder clinging to her now. "It was understandable," he assured her, "given the fact Miss Sadie's identity had been stolen. For all you knew, I was the thief come to cause even more mischief."

The timer dinged, and Noelle pivoted toward the microwave. She peered inside, checked the contents of the dinners and started the oven up again. "Is Miss Sadie going to be liable for the massive amount of debt whoever did this ran up in her name?"

Kevin noted it seemed important to Noelle that Miss Sadie not suffer. That alone proved nothing. A lot of white collar criminals felt they were stealing from businesses that were reimbursed by insurance companies, not people, and therefore justified it on some level because the victim was a faceless corporation.

Kevin tackled the last stack of mail. "On Miss Sadie's own credit cards, there's probably a set limit she'll be liable for, possibly as low as fifty dollars, depending on the terms of her agreement with the bank that issued them. But she won't be liable for the cards that were fraudulently applied for and issued during her absence. Unfortunately, it is going to take awhile to prove that was done by someone other than Miss Sadie herself, and get all this straightened out…and during that time her name is going to be mud at all the banks. It looks like she is maxed out on all her current cards."

Noelle filled two glasses with ice and water. "How can this happen?"

Kevin leaned back in his chair and watched her slice up a lemon. It was a simple domestic act, yet it filled him with pleasure. "Someone got hold of Miss Sadie's personal information, signed her up for cards and used a Houston post office box as her mailing address," he explained. "Once the cards were issued and activated, it looks like the thieves began ordering goods off the Internet and had them delivered as "gifts" to other people at post office boxes around the state."

Noelle's brow furrowed. "Shouldn't someone have figured this out?" she complained.

Kevin noted that this woman was either innocent of any wrongdoing, or an Oscar-caliber actress. He leaned back as she put the beverage in front of him. "Obviously, given the volume of letters Miss Sadie received at her permanent Laramie and Houston addresses, people were questioning what was going on and putting holds on various accounts until they heard from her. Unfortunately, because she was on her cruise, no one was able to reach her. It looks like most of the activity took place in a three-week period at the end of November. Do you know what day she left on her cruise?" he asked curiously.

Noelle nodded. She plucked silverware out of one drawer, napkins from another. "October twenty-ninth. I met with her right before she left."

"And she got back…?" Aware they were about to eat, Kevin moved the stacks of sorted mail out of the way.

"Three days ago," Noelle replied. "Miss Sadie spent the night in Houston, then picked up her mail at the nearby post office the following morning. She had her regular driver bring her out to Laramie, where she stopped at the post office, picked up that mail, and headed out here to Blackberry Hill. She said she waited until she got to the house to start going through it all, so she had no idea what was going on."

The microwave dinged again. Noelle removed the dinners from the oven and handed him the beef and broccoli, keeping the lemon chicken and broccoli for herself. They peeled off the plastic covers. Steam curled through the air, giving the kitchen a distinctive Asian aroma.

"How are you going to track the thieves?" Noelle asked, taking a seat opposite Kevin.

"I'm going to start by talking to everyone close to Miss Sadie, and have her fill out some forms about who works in her home, or on the property, or has occasion to see her private papers. Whoever did this had to have access to her birth date, social security number, bank information and so on. In all likelihood it's someone close to her she would never suspect, which is why I'm going to be taking a hard look at the background of everyone around her."

Noelle seemed nervous again. "Couldn't it have been a stranger?" she asked, a troubled look in her eyes.

Kevin struggled to contain his disappointment. He did not want Noelle to have anything to do with this. "It could have been," he agreed carefully.

She released the breath she had been holding. "But you don't think it is." She kept her eyes on his.

Kevin debated how much to tell her. "I find the timing odd," he said finally. "Miss Sadie goes off for a six-week cruise, and two days later, a flurry of bank card applications are entered in her name. She has a stellar credit rating, so the cards are issued promptly—probably all within hours of each other. Ten days later, purchases begin. And then magically stop right before she gets home from her cruise. Common sense says it was no accident that this happened while she was out of touch."

Noelle's expression turned contemplative. She put her fork down and dabbed the corners of her mouth with her napkin. "So what next?"

I try like hell to remain objective. "I talk to my friends in Houston who specialize in identity theft for the HPD. There may be others in the area who are reporting similar fraud."

"Maybe people on the same cruise?" Noelle asked hopefully.

Clearly, she was looking for an easy solution to the puzzle. "Or people who all used the same travel agency to book vacations. Then again, a common thread could be people whose homes are all monitored by the same security company, companies that would have been informed of the prolonged absence of the residents. And we can't rule out that it could be an isolated incident—just someone close to Miss Sadie who wanted to give their family a good Christmas."

Noelle picked up her fork and toyed with her food once again. "I find it hard to believe anyone close to Miss Sadie would do this to her," she said stubbornly.

"You prefer the stranger angle."

"Yes."

So did he, truth be known. However, Kevin

had learned the hard way that not everyone could be trusted. "Desperation makes people do awful things."

Noelle shook her head in frustration. "But to take advantage of an eighty-five-year-old woman who is one of the sweetest, most generous people I've ever met…"

"I agree. It's awful. But I can't let my personal feelings for Miss Sadie hamper my investigation, which is why I'm going to take a hard look at everyone around Miss Sadie." Kevin paused. "Including," he said meaningfully, looking straight at her, "you."

NOELLE HAD EXPECTED she would be investigated, given all Kevin had just said about the likely suspect being someone with easy proximity to Miss Sadie. She hadn't expected it to hurt so much. Temper igniting, she pushed away from the table and headed to the sink. "Don't forget Dash."

Kevin finished his meal. "I won't."

"Or my son, Mikey," Noelle continued

heatedly, dumping the remains of her dinner into the disposal, her appetite gone. "He could have done it, too."

Kevin dropped his own black plastic dish into the trash and carried the silverware over to the dishwasher. "You're offended."

Noelle glared at him. "I'd like to say I understand you're just doing your job."

He took the disposable dish out of her hand and threw it away, too. "But you can't." He turned back to face her.

Trying not to notice how fit and handsome he looked in his starched khaki uniform, Noelle shook her head. "No. I can't. I don't like being accused of something I did not do." It brought back too many memories of a time she would rather forget.

He gave her a steady, assessing look.

Noelle jerked in a breath, aware she had inadvertently revealed too much. To her relief, the front door opened and then closed.

Seconds later, Dash strolled into the kitchen. "Sorry it took me so long to get here," he told

Kevin. "I wanted to stay until I was sure that Aunt Sadie was settled for the night." He glanced at Noelle. "Were you able to find all the paperwork Detective McCabe needed?"

Kevin lifted a hand, interrupting, "You can both call me Kevin."

"I don't know if that is such a good idea," Noelle interjected coolly. Temper still simmering, she looked at Dash, confiding, "It seems we're all suspects in the identity theft."

"As it should be," Dash replied, obviously in total agreement. He crossed to Noelle's side and put a companionable arm about her shoulders. "Not that it will take Kevin long to eliminate you." He grinned, switching from lawyer mode to Southern charm in the time it took to draw a breath. "Me, on the other hand, well, we all know what a disreputable character I am."

Noelle smiled. Dash was one of the most honest, caring men she had ever met. He also knew the secrets of her past. If he didn't think she had anything to worry about, she probably didn't. Getting his silent message to relax and let things unfold as they would, she forced the tension from her limbs.

His mood abruptly all-business, Kevin gathered up the papers on the end of the table. "Do you want to make copies for me now, or drop them off at the station tomorrow?"

Noelle hesitated. Neither option appealed to her.

"I'll do it right now on Aunt Sadie's copier in the study upstairs," Dash said. He looked at Noelle with easy familiarity.

"Thanks," Noelle said quietly, glad for the help.

"No problem. Any chance I could get a mug of very strong coffee before I hit the road?"

Noelle had expected Dash would not stay in Laramie for long. Still, she was disappointed. She could have used someone to run interference between her and Kevin. Thus far, Dash had proved very adept at it. "You have to go back to Houston tonight?"

He nodded. "I've got to be in court again tomorrow, so I'll need to leave as soon as I get these copied for Kevin. Be right back." He exited the kitchen.

Once again, Noelle and Kevin were alone. Noelle could feel him sizing her up. Trying to figure out the exact nature of her relationship with Dash. Maybe it was petty of her, but she hoped he stayed confused.

"Is there anyone in Houston you think I might need to investigate?" Kevin asked matter-of-factly.

"Besides me and Dash, you mean?" Noelle retorted sweetly.

He waited, unsmiling.

Okay, she was overreacting, given the circumstances. But darn it all, Kevin didn't know what she had been through in the years before she had been rescued by Dash and his legal expertise. "I can't think of anyone," she said finally, forcing herself to remain detached.

"Thanks, anyway."

Noelle made a show of wiping down the table. "I do have a question."

He leaned against the counter. "Fire away."

Wishing she weren't so aware of his presence, Noelle retreated into scrupulous politeness. "I'd like to get the steps repaired and painted before

Christmas. Do you know of anyone who could do it for me on short notice?"

Kevin nodded. "I'll have someone here tomorrow evening to tear down the rotten wood. The steps can be rebuilt Saturday morning, a coat of waterproofing put on. Primer and paint can be applied the following day—as long as the weather holds and there is no rain."

That would certainly take care of it. "Thank you," Noelle said grudgingly.

"In return, I want something from you."

It figured. "You're kidding," she said sarcastically.

He held out his hands, palm up. "Nothing in life is free."

Especially when it came to Kevin McCabe. "What do you want?" she demanded, on edge again.

"The sheriff's department organizes a Blue Santa operation every year. It's a good cause. A lot of residents volunteer. We gather up toys and donations of food and clothing that are distributed to the needy throughout the county. We schedule an exciting appearance by Santa. For the record, I got tapped for that this year."

Now that would be something to see. "Should have kept your beard," she taunted lightly. "Although you would have had to do something to make it white."

He let her remarks pass. "We also hand out presents to the kids and gift baskets for the adults, and then we have a potluck dinner for everyone— volunteers, their families and the folks we help— over at the community center on the evening of December twenty-third."

Noelle was impressed despite herself. "That sounds laudable."

"And fun. Anyway, every year we split up the work. Because I was out of town fishing for the first two weeks of the drive, I ended up being responsible for two things, in addition to playing Santa. The decorations for the dinner…"

Noelle shrugged, aware that every time she got near him, her heart beat faster, her senses got sharper and the isolation she'd felt since her husband's death became a little more acute. She thought she had been living fully. Obviously, she hadn't been.

Deciding she had looked into Kevin's eyes far too long, she turned away once again. "That doesn't sound too hard."

He watched her wipe down the counters and the inside of the microwave. "Maybe not for you," he chided. "You make your living putting together events."

Promising herself she was not going to fall prey to the attraction simmering between them, she forced her gaze back to the rugged contours of his face. "What's the second thing?"

His mouth flattened into a grim line. "Baby doll revitalization."

She couldn't help it. She began to laugh.

His eyes narrowed. "It's not funny. People are very generous about donating. And we appreciate it, as do the kids who receive the gifts. But some of these dolls aren't in the best of shape, to put it lightly. And I'm in charge of making sure they all seem like new."

Noelle looked him up and down. "I can see this would be tough for you."

Kevin rolled his eyes in exasperation. "You have no idea."

"Didn't spend a lot of time playing with dolls when you were a kid?"

"Can't say that I did. I'm begging you to help me out."

Twisting her arm was more like it. "There must be someone else you could ask," Noelle replied. "A sister, mother, some woman who is terribly interested in you."

"True—except they've already volunteered and are set to help out in various other ways."

"Maybe they wouldn't mind taking on another task."

"But then I'd owe them," Kevin retorted, as if that would be the worst thing in the world.

"And you wouldn't owe me?" Noelle asked curiously.

"Not if I fix Miss Sadie's steps for you. Then we'd be even."

"Whoa. Who said anything about you repairing the steps?" Noelle said.

"I did." He palmed his chest. "I'm a very handy carpenter, and truth be told, I feel a little bad about the way that all unfolded. This way, if I fix what I helped you break, I don't have to feel guilty."

"Or worry about your karma," Noelle guessed, trying not to be amused...and failing mightily.

"Right."

She blew out a gusty breath. "You are one complicated man."

"So what do you say?" He moved closer, hands spread, and blasted her with a hopeful smile. "Do we have a deal?"

Noelle had never been one to swoon over a man in uniform, but there was no denying Kevin McCabe made an impression she was not likely to forget. One minute he was saving her and her son from sure injury, the next flirting. The man practically exuded honor, audaciousness and the determination to do right no matter what the cost. She didn't know what he was up to now, but didn't like it one bit.

Clearly aware he was annoying her terribly, he looked her over from head to toe, taking in the delicate hollow of her throat and the shadowy hint of cleavage in the open V of her white shirt. His gaze moved lower still to check out the fit of her tailored slacks before returning to her eyes. "You're very sure of yourself." She regarded him perceptively.

He gazed back with a charming smile, still holding her gaze. "Not so sure."

The way he looked at her then—as if he was thinking what it might be like to make love to her—sent tremors of awareness tumbling through her. "What do you mean?" Noelle demanded, hanging on to her composure by a thread.

"For example—" he leaned toward her conspiratorially "—I'm not certain you want to kiss me, but your body language says you do."

"Detective." Noelle lifted her chin, drew a deep breath. "You're not really thinking of putting the moves on me just now." She inched back.

"Not thinking." He stepped toward her, laced his hands around her waist and tugged her against him.

"Which is," he continued thoughtfully, looking down at her intently, "perhaps the problem."

KEVIN HAD KNOWN he was in trouble the minute he accepted Noelle's dinner invitation and entered the cozy confines of the kitchen. But he'd done it anyway, hoping the casual intimacy of the situation would seduce her into revealing all sorts of things about herself and her relationship with Dash and Miss Sadie. Kevin figured he could put his considerable attraction to her aside long enough to investigate her connection, or lack thereof, to the case he was working on. He'd intended to figure out why he had seen flashes of guilt and fear in her eyes whenever the subject of the identity theft came up.

However, he hadn't expected to see raw vulnerability in her eyes in her most unguarded moments. She had the same hunted, despairing look the bullied kids had always had in school. The look that said they knew they had done nothing to deserve the treatment they were getting, but were braced to suffer all sorts of indignities anyway. Kevin had never been able to stand by while an underdog was suffering then, and he couldn't do it now. To his chagrin, he found himself wanting to protect Noelle, not investigate her. He found himself wanting to get closer. Not as law enforcement. As a man. He found himself wanting to satisfy her obvious desire to be kissed. To bring her closer yet. To investigate the softness of her lips....

Noelle saw the kiss coming and could have avoided it, if she had wanted to. She didn't. Maybe because this was the kind of kiss she had always dreamed about and never received. Gentle. Tender. Evocative. Maybe because she had known instinctively that the touch of his lips to hers would rock her to the core. And the reality was even better than she had ever imagined. Noelle was inundated with so many sensations at once. The hard warmth of his body. The yummy taste of his mouth. The clean masculine fragrance of his skin. Heavens, the man knew how to kiss, she thought, letting herself be drawn into the erotic moment. He knew how to exact a sensual response from her. Knew how to make her want and need. Knew how to…draw back.

Startled, she hitched in a breath and stared into his eyes. To her surprise, he looked as taken aback as she felt. Who knew what would have happened next had it not been for the sound of swift footsteps overhead, forcing them farther apart? Seconds later, Dash bounded down the back stairs, two stacks of papers in hand, one of which he handed to Kevin. "I made two copies of everything, one for me, one for you. The originals will stay here with Miss Sadie."

"Good thinking," Kevin said.

Dash smiled at Noelle, his presence effectively breaking the mood. "Coffee ready?" he asked cheerfully.

Noelle feigned normalcy. "It will be in a minute." Just as soon as she put it on.

Kevin looked at Noelle, no sign of what had transpired between them on his handsome face. Instead, he seemed to be wondering what had come over him, as surely as she was wondering what had come over her! "I better be going, too," he said.

Her throat dry, she nodded. "I'll tell Miss Sadie you're working hard to solve her case."

"And I'll tell her you've agreed to help with the Blue Santa holiday drive this year. That will please her. She's one of our biggest contributors."

Except I didn't quite agree, Noelle thought as Dash walked Kevin to the front door before returning to the kitchen. *You just sort of volunteered me. And I was too distracted to say no....*

"Nice guy," Dash remarked, returning to her side.

Complicated. And Noelle had always had a thing for complicated men, even though she rarely acted on it.

"And dedicated," Dash continued.

"Not to mention suspicious," Noelle said out loud, meeting Dash's eyes. Telling herself she had to work harder to keep her defenses in place, she got out the coffee and filters. She could not end up flirting with Kevin McCabe again. Never mind kissing!

"You're worried he'll find out about your stay in juvie?" Dash guessed.

Her spine stiffening at the memory of that awful

time in her life, Noelle put beans in the grinder and turned it on. "As well as what happened after I got out."

Dash shrugged. "You could just tell him."

And have Kevin McCabe look at her the way others had when they'd found out she'd spent time in lockup? "No. I'm not going back there, Dash, not even in my thoughts." She looked him straight in the eye. "Not ever again."

"So how are things out at Blackberry Hill?" Rio asked when Kevin walked into the station.

As out of control as ever, Kevin thought. What had gotten into him, anyway? Seducing a woman he had yet to eliminate as a suspect? He had meant to catch her off guard and get her to open up a little bit this evening. Instead, he had ended up letting *his* guard down, flirting, allowing the simmering attraction between them to flare up. He had given in to impulse and actually kissed her. And there had been nothing official at all about that move. That had been pure desire on his part. Passion was not something that typically drove his actions. He had much more control over himself than that. And yet there was something about Noelle Kringle that drew him like a bee to nectar. Despite her made-up name.

He had to do better.

Rio elbowed him in the side. "Did you ride off again somewhere? 'Cause you sure look like you're standing here."

"Sorry." Kevin set the stack of papers on his desk and powered up his computer.

Rio went back to his hunt-and-peck typing. "I should be making you write up this danged report," he complained, "since you're the one who caused the problem this afternoon."

Everyone knew how much Rio hated paperwork. Although, in Kevin's estimation, his colleague made the process much more painful than it had to be by procrastinating forever before getting down to business. Of course, Kevin admitted, that was probably due to the fact that, like him, Rio had no one to go home to after work. Sometimes being single in a two-by-two world really bit. Never more so than during the holidays, which was why Kevin had decided to stop feeling sorry about the lack of a wife and kids in his life and go off fishing for the first half of December. So he wouldn't have to think about the glaring void in his existence.

"You look more unhappy than I do." Rio stopped typing abruptly and got up. He went over to refill his coffee cup with a brew that was thick as molasses and had all the aromatic qualities of used motor oil.

"I see you made the coffee again," Kevin noted.

Overhearing, several of the other deputies chuckled.

Rio perched on the edge of Kevin's desk. He took a sip of coffee and somehow managed not to wince. "So how long are Miss Sadie's nephew and that babe—what was her name again—?"

Like Rio didn't know. "Noelle Kringle," Kevin said, for the benefit of everyone else in the room.

"—going to be around?" Rio finished curiously.

Kevin checked his e-mail and found 228 messages waiting for him. After deciding to get caught up later on what had happened while he was on vacation, he moved his cursor to the Background Check function. "Dash Nelson was going to head back to Houston this evening." Kevin couldn't say he was sorry about that. It would be a heck of a lot easier to investigate Noelle without her protector around.

"And what about Noelle?"

Kevin pushed aside the memory of her incredibly soft lips...and how sweet they had tasted. He had a job to do that did not include kissing her—or even dreaming about doing so—again. "I'm not sure how long she's going to be here." He got up to get himself some awful coffee. "At least a few more days." Until the side entry steps were finished, he guessed.

"Is she hooked up with Dash?" Rio asked when Kevin had sat back down again.

"Not sure." He took a sip and found the coffee as hot and bitter as he had expected. "There's definitely an intimacy between them."

Rio's eyes lit up curiously, along with every other deputy's in the room. "Sexual?"

Kevin shook his head. "Not that I saw, anyway.

Dash Nelson treats her more like a wife he's had around for a while and sort of relies on to fetch and carry."

"Hmm." Rio studied him. "You calling dibs on this one?"

Guilt swept through Kevin, even as he denied the possibility. "Rio, I'm investigating her."

"So?" He shrugged. "I assume you'll clear her eventually."

Kevin hoped so. Otherwise, he was headed down a road he had traveled before, hankering after a woman who was nothing more than a very accomplished criminal.

Rio's eyes gleamed cynically. He knew why Kevin was so reluctant to get involved on a personal level. "Did you run a background check on her yet?"

"I'm about to." Kevin typed in the appropriate commands and waited. No Prior Arrests flashed on the screen. There wasn't so much as a single traffic ticket attached to her record.

"That ought to make you feel better," Rio said, reading over his shoulder.

Kevin lifted a brow.

"I assume you would prefer—as would I—that whoever did this to Miss Sadie be a stranger, rather than a close and trusted acquaintance or family friend?"

Kevin knew what he meant. It felt less invasive if the perpetrator of a crime was someone who had selected a victim at random. If the injured party knew it was nothing personal. Because when the "mark" knew the perpetrator of the crime, and trusted or loved the person, it was pure torture.

Rio slapped Kevin on the shoulder. "So Merry Christmas, partner. You're free to pursue her."

Kevin thought about Noelle Kringle's less than innocent reaction and then scoffed, his emotional armor back in place. "Are you kidding?" He wasn't pursuing anything until he knew exactly who he was dealing with. "I'm just getting started."

Chapter Four

"So what'd you find out?" Rio asked the following afternoon.

Kevin leaned back in his desk chair. "Noelle Kringle was born and reared in Houston. Her parents were Bert and Norma Smith. They died eight years ago in an automobile accident, when Noelle was just nineteen. Bert was an electrical engineer, employed with the same company for twenty years. Her mother was a homemaker. The family owned one modest home in Houston that has since been torn down to make way for a shopping mall." Which made it impossible to go and talk to any of the Smiths' former neighbors— easily, anyway. "There's nothing to report on any of them. No traffic tickets, criminal records, legal disputes or credit problems. Nothing on her late husband, Michael Kringle, Sr., either."

"How about Miss Sadie's nephew?"

"Dash Nelson is a respected member of the Texas bar, an ace litigator who also does a lot of pro bono work for disadvantaged youths. He's got plenty of money of his own, and a close relationship with his aunt, so there's no motive there. If he wanted or needed money from Miss Sadie, all he would have to do is ask."

Rio pulled up a chair. "What financial shape is Noelle Kringle in?"

"Not great." Aware that Noelle had had a harder time than she let on, Kevin frowned. "Her parents left her only a few thousand dollars when they died, after their estate was settled. She worked minimum wage jobs—waitress, banquet server—before getting on with a catering firm as an event planner. She stopped working for that company when she married, and became self-employed, doing solo events for Miss Sadie and several other prominent families. She lives in a town home in a respectable neighborhood with her son. Her bank account shows no unusual activity. She seems to have enough to get by, but nothing that would indicate she's involved in any kind of scam."

"So she's off your suspect list?" Rio asked.

"Not quite."

Rio cocked a brow.

"Something about her just doesn't feel right," Kevin added.

"You think she's a crook?"

Kevin's wary nature kicked in. "I think she's hiding something."

"Like…?" his buddy pressed.

Kevin shrugged and stood, feeling ready for action once again. "I don't know. But I'm going to find out," he vowed. "It's the only way I'll be able to rule her out as a suspect, once and for all."

NOELLE WAS SITTING at Miss Sadie's bedside, finishing up the latest round of notes for the parties Miss Sadie was planning to have in Laramie, when Kevin McCabe strolled in.

He was in full uniform again today. The starched khaki shirt and dark brown pants molded his athletic frame. He'd had a haircut and a shave. The faint hint of cologne clung to his skin. Her pulse quickened as their eyes locked, and then it leaped again as he hunkered down and gently greeted her son. "How you doing, sport?" Kevin said as he watched the boy play with his cars and trucks on a race track rug Noelle had brought in.

Mikey lifted the truck in his hand for Kevin to see. "Tick-up-puck!" The little boy looked at him, obviously wanting to be sure Kevin understood what he had said.

Noelle noted with amusement that the deputy hadn't a clue.

"Mikey is showing you his pickup truck." Noelle enunciated carefully, for benefit of her toddler son.

Recognition dawned. "That is a very nice pickup truck," he agreed emphatically, looking Mikey straight in the eye.

The little boy beamed.

Kevin patted him gently on the shoulder, then stood up again.

The mood shifted as electricity arced between

him and Noelle, generated no doubt by the memory of that sizzling kiss they had shared. She did her best to ignore it. As did he.

Smiling, Miss Sadie looked at the large cloth sack Kevin held in one hand. "What have you got there?"

He shrugged, his attention focused now on the genteel elderly woman. "A little elf told me you and some of the other ladies here at Laramie Gardens know how to sew."

Miss Sadie nodded. "Why, yes, we do. It was an art taught to all the ladies of my generation. It was part of the school curriculum."

Relief etched his handsome features and he handed her the sack. "We have a lot of baby doll clothing in need of tender loving care. And time is short, I'm afraid."

Miss Sadie plucked a torn dress from the bag. "I see what you mean."

Kevin regarded her hopefully. "Any chance I could get you to be in charge of the task, Miss Sadie?"

"Consider it done, Deputy McCabe. When did you need them?"

"By the morning of the twenty-third? That would give us the afternoon to get the dolls put back together and ready to give out to the children."

"I'll talk to the other ladies at dinner this evening."

She handed the bag back and Kevin set it in the corner, out of harm's way.

"Now," Miss Sadie continued, "what have you been able to find out about my identity theft since we spoke yesterday?"

Kevin's expression grew serious. "What happened to you was part of a big, elaborate scam, Miss Sadie. Twenty-five other Houston families, all socially and financially prominent, were hit. Same M.O. for all of them. New credit card accounts were opened. In some situations, the victims were traveling. In others, accounts were begun under the name of a person in a nursing home, or at a college." He folded his arms in front of him. "Multiple e-mail accounts were then set up in each victim's name on free e-mail servers on the Web, and goods were ordered from there as 'holiday gifts' for other people. Three addresses were used as drops for the goods—all rental houses whose residents have since moved out, if they ever really moved in. The ordered merchandise is probably being sold, or used to get store credit, as we speak."

"Can you track it?" Miss Sadie asked.

"Not easily," Kevin replied regretfully, "given the fact it's the Christmas season, and much of the merchandise ordered on your account was for things like watches and iPods and laptop computers that are sold in high volume this time of year, anyway. But we are tracking the origin of the e-mail accounts. The host companies have pinpointed a public library close to a university in southwest Houston where the requests for credit cards originated, and they've set up a sting there to catch anyone who might come back to continue their criminal activity."

Miss Sadie pressed a frail hand to her throat. "Well, that's good to know. Isn't it, Noelle?"

"Yes." Noelle looked Kevin straight in the eye, letting him know once again she had absolutely nothing to feel guilty about. "It is."

"Thieves simply should not be able to operate

during the Christmas season," Miss Sadie declared emotionally. "And speaking of the holiday, did you hear my news?" she asked Kevin.

He shook his head.

"I've talked Noelle and little Mikey into spending the Christmas holiday with me at Blackberry Hill!" she announced enthusiastically. She clapped her hands and glanced at Noelle. "Dash is going to be so pleased when he hears you'll be joining us this year for the entire event."

Mikey stopped playing long enough to clap his hands, too. They all laughed. He grinned and clapped again, before returning to his trucks.

"I can't wait to tell Dash this evening," Miss Sadie said.

Noelle flushed. She didn't know what it was about the yuletide season, but it seemed like everybody wanted all single people to be hooked up. She wondered if Kevin McCabe was getting the same pressure from his family and friends.

Eyes twinkling, Kevin scratched his ear.

"Sounds like you're doing a little matchmaking there, Miss Sadie."

"I admit I wouldn't mind if the two of them finally stopped dawdling and made a match," Miss Sadie replied with customary frankness. "In fact, I can't think of a better Christmas present for me."

Noelle cleared her throat. "Back to your investigation, Deputy McCabe," she said in a low, strangled voice, ignoring the faint hint of disappointment in his eyes. She was not taking advantage of Dash and Miss Sadie! "What else is being done to wrap this investigation up as soon as possible?" she queried, making it clear that she wanted the thieves caught as desperately as Miss Sadie did.

His expression all-business, Kevin directed his answer to both women. "The rest of the families are filling out the same questionnaire I brought you this morning, Miss Sadie. When we get them all back in, we'll be comparing them, looking for similarities."

"Such as…?" Noelle asked.

"What event planners and caterers they used."

Okay, now he was really getting under her skin, Noelle decided. She leveled a warning glance his way and thought she saw a glimmer of amusement in his eyes.

"Surely you're not hinting that Noelle had anything to do with this!" Miss Sadie declared, incensed.

"I'm not hinting anything," Kevin said. "I'm just explaining the way a theft investigation works.

Baloney, Noelle thought. "Don't let him fool you, Miss Sadie. He's investigating me. He told me as much last evening."

Miss Sadie lifted an indignant brow. "That really isn't necessary, Detective."

"I'm afraid it is." Kevin watched Mikey drive his pickup truck across the floor. "I'd be remiss in my duty if I left any stone unturned. Although you'll both be glad to know—" Kevin smiled as Mikey passed him and continued toward his mom "—Miss Kringle appears completely innocent thus far."

"I could have told you that," Miss Sadie huffed.

"Don't fault him for doing his job," Noelle soothed. She reached down to pick up her son and hold him on her lap. "Detective McCabe has to look at everyone if he hopes to find the culprit."

"I'm glad you understand," Kevin replied as Mikey wreathed both arms around his mother's neck and rested his head on her shoulder.

She stroked his downy curls. "I do understand." It didn't mean she didn't resent it.

"Hungee, Momma," Mikey interrupted, with quiet urgency.

Guilt flowed through Noelle as she realized time had gotten away from her. "Oh, goodness," she said, consulting her watch. "It's dinnertime." She stood with Mikey cradled on her hip, and began gathering up her things.

Kevin helped by retrieving toys and slipping them into her diaper bag. "I'll walk you out," he said, taking the child in his arms while she put on her coat, and then Mikey's, too.

"Thank you," she said grudgingly before taking Mikey over to kiss Miss Sadie goodbye. "We'll see you tomorrow," she promised.

"I'm looking forward to it." Miss Sadie beamed. Kevin bid her adieu, too.

"I don't suppose I could get you to look at the community center this evening," he said as they left the building and walked toward Noelle's white van.

She hit the remote button on her keypad and heard the locks click open. After Kevin got the side door, she settled Mikey in his car seat. "I already looked at it earlier this afternoon and took notes. As soon as you tell me what budget you have in terms of decorations, I'll let you know what I think you should do."

Kevin watched while she made sure the safety strap was centered just right across Mikey's chest. "How about we discuss it over dinner?"

Noelle handed her son his blanket and a book to "read" while she drove. "I can't get a sitter."

"Bring Mikey with us. Mi Casa Mexican Restaurant is right down the street."

Noelle shut the rear door and climbed behind the wheel. This man sure was persistent. As were a lot of men, when it came to wanting her to go out with them. What was different about this was that she actually wanted to go. Keeping her guard up, she smiled up at him pleasantly. "Mikey doesn't eat Tex-Mex."

"Doesn't have to. They have a children's menu with all the standard items. Grilled cheese, hot dogs, hamburgers, chicken fingers and fries."

"Fries!" Mikey echoed eagerly from the back.

Noelle knew time was of the essence if she didn't want to have a meltdown on her hands. Still… "Mikey can be a rather impatient diner, especially when he's tired and didn't have much of a nap, as was the case today."

Kevin shrugged. "Luckily for us all, I can be very patient."

"Fries!" Mikey said again, even more urgently.

Oh, what the heck… "You're paying?" Noelle said, just to get under his skin.

"Of course." He shut her door, then waited until she started the van and put down her window. "I am a gentleman."

Noelle snorted, aware they were flirting again, even though they really shouldn't be. "Could have fooled me last night," she muttered, snapping her own safety belt into place.

His eyes held hers. "Because I kissed you."

And had me kissing you back, Noelle thought, aware how just thinking about that embrace made her tingle. "That can't happen again," she warned.

Kevin smiled and made no reply.

"I'M CURIOUS," Kevin said as soon as they had placed their orders—beef fajitas for him, sour cream chicken enchiladas for her.

"Now, that's a surprise," Noelle quipped.

The waiter brought out Mikey's dinner in advance of theirs, as requested.

"Just what is your relationship with Dash Nelson?" Kevin asked, watching the sparks come into her pretty eyes.

Noelle handed Mikey his sippy cup of milk, then concentrated on cutting up the grilled cheese sandwich and fries into toddler-size pieces. Kevin knew he had annoyed her, but her voice was relaxed. "We're just friends."

Mikey put down his cup and pushed grilled

cheese bites into his mouth with the flat of his palm. When the toddler dropped one on his lap, Kevin reached over to help him retrieve it. "Miss Sadie seems to want you married," he observed.

Noelle cut up a few green beans, too. "That doesn't mean it's going to happen."

Kevin watched Mikey arrange and rearrange his food on the child-size plate in front of him, all the while taking occasional spoonfuls of applesauce from his mother. "Are the two of you dating?"

This earned him the reproving look he expected. "No," Noelle stated clearly, letting him know she did not appreciate his probing. Not all of which, Kevin admitted ruefully to himself, was police-work related. "Not that it's any of your business," she finished, shifting in her chair and inadvertently nudging one of his knees under the table.

It was if he intended to pursue her. Or if— worst case scenario—what she turned out to be hiding from him was somehow relevant to his ongoing investigation. "But you do go out together." Kevin shifted, too, so they wouldn't be crowding each other.

Noelle handed Mikey a green bean. "From time to time, yes. Platonically." She leaned back to let the waiter put her plate of steaming food in front of her.

"And Dash doesn't want anything more," Kevin pressed, surprised to find he was a little jealous of the proximity the successful attorney enjoyed to the beautiful woman across from him.

Satisfied that Mikey was well-occupied with his own food, she began to eat her enchiladas. "Dash knows how much I loved my husband, how devastated I was when Michael died."

Kevin could see it was true. "That doesn't mean Dash doesn't want you for himself, or already assumes he has your total devotion," he remarked, layering sizzling strips of beef, pepper and onion in a warm flour tortilla.

"What makes you think that?" she asked.

Kevin met her eyes. "The way you fixed coffee for him the other night before he hit the road. He appears to take you for granted, the way married couples do each other."

Noelle sipped her iced tea slowly, then put her glass down. "If that's the case, it's a two-way street, since I guess I have depended on him in some ways ever since my husband died."

Because Dash served as extended family, Kevin wondered, or because he effectively kept other men away? Noelle's emotional reaction to his question suggested that he hadn't been the first to hint that this setup was not a good situation for either her or Dash.

"You're sure you want to work on the steps tonight?" Noelle asked a short time later, after settling Mikey back in his car seat.

Although she had been very polite during the rest of their meal, Kevin knew she would like nothing better than to get rid of him now. Unfortunately, he had committed to help her and Miss Sadie with the repair…and McCabes always kept their promises. "You know what they say—never put off until tomorrow what you can do today," he replied, aware he had another motive as well. He was hoping she would stop being ticked off at him before the evening's end. And that reaction puzzled him, too. Usually he didn't care whether the people he was investigating liked him or not.

The drive took twenty minutes. Kevin followed Noelle and used the time to check his voice mail messages, on his cell and at the station. To his relief, all calls related to other investigations or family matters. No incriminating information on Noelle. Which meant, he hoped, that his gut instinct was right. She might be hiding something from him, but she was no threat to Miss Sadie, or others in the Houston community.

When they arrived at Blackberry Hill, Kevin parked behind Noelle and got out. By the time he reached the van, she was already trying to get a diaper bag, her purse and a rather uncooperative Mikey out of the vehicle. "Want me to take something for you?" Kevin asked.

"Play!" Mikey demanded, squirming in Noelle's arms. "Now!"

"No, honey, it's dark and cold out here. We have to go inside," Noelle said firmly.

Mikey let out a rebel yell and promptly went limp in her arms.

Noelle sagged under twenty-eight pounds of dead weight.

Kevin slid his arms beneath hers and lifted. Mikey was so surprised that he forgot to stay limp. "Thanks," Noelle said.

"Want me to carry him the rest of the way?"

Still struggling to catch her breath, she relinquished the recalcitrant toddler. "If you wouldn't mind…"

"So, Mikey. Guess you've had a pretty long day," Kevin observed as they strolled toward the house.

Noelle had her key ready when they reached the front steps. Made of the same pink brick as the mansion, they were probably sturdy enough to last a hundred years, Kevin mused, eyeing them critically.

As they crossed the porch, Mikey put his thumb in his mouth and stared at Kevin consideringly.

"Mikey, it's time for your bath," Noelle said as they entered the foyer.

Another rebel yell. Louder than the first.

Noelle looked at her son, maternal love fighting with exhaustion in her eyes. Mikey wasn't the only one who'd had a long day, Kevin noted. "If you want me to help, I'll be glad to lend a hand," he said.

"You're serious." She seemed stunned.

Kevin shrugged. "Nothing I haven't done before for my nephews and nieces. My sibs don't hesitate to put me into service."

"Then you're on," Noelle agreed. "Could you sit and entertain him for a few minutes while I run his bath and get out his pajamas?"

"No problem."

Mikey picked up a plastic tow truck similar to the one he had been playing with earlier. "T'uck," he told Kevin soberly. "Tuck-up-pick."

Half an hour later, Mikey was bathed and ready for bed. Noelle brought out a cookie shaped like a banana, a sippy cup of milk and a Christmas story about a black-and-white dog. Kevin, seeing all was in order, went to change into his work clothes. When he came out of the guest bathroom, Noelle was reading "'Twas the Night before Christmas" to Mikey. Seeing Kevin, the child eased out of her lap, picked his half-eaten cookie off the plastic dish and toddled over to Kevin. He held it up. "Eat!"

Kevin hunkered down, not sure what it was

about this kid and his mother that got to him. He only knew that when they were near he couldn't take his eyes off either of them. "Thank you! Mmm!" He pretended to nibble on the treat.

Mikey pushed it against his lips. "Eat!" he demanded.

Kevin looked at an amused Noelle. "Up to you," she said. "But he knows the difference between really doing something and pretending to do it."

Kevin took a small bite off one end and gave the rest back to him. Mikey chortled in delight, then ran to his mother and pushed what remained of the cookie at her lips.

"Mmm!" she said, taking the offered gift. "Thank you, honey. Finish your milk and then say good night and thank you to Kevin."

Mikey took a drink, then looked at Kevin. "You're welcome!" he chirped.

"Anytime." Kevin winked.

Appreciating what a tender sight mother and son made, he ruffled Mikey's hair and waved good-night as Noelle carried him toward the stairs. More aware than ever of what was missing in his life, Kevin headed out to his truck to get his tools. Okay, so he didn't have a wife and kids of his own to love. But he still had a lot to be thankful for, he reminded himself sternly, refusing to give in to the holiday blues. He needed to get busy, not stand around lusting after the sexiest, most enticing woman he had ever kissed.

Forty-five minutes later, he had ripped off all the rotten boards and stacked them in the back of his SUV for transport to the dump, when Noelle came around the corner of the house, serving tray in hand. She had put on her black wool coat and ivory cashmere scarf, and her copper curls made a tousled halo about her face.

"Oh, my!" she exclaimed, seeing the progress he'd made.

Kevin grinned, amazed at how happy she made him just by being herself. He had to wrap this investigation up fast, so he would be free to explore what was developing between them. "Not much left, is there?" he murmured, ambling toward her.

"There isn't!" She paused to look where the wooden steps had been.

Kevin ripped off his work gloves and stuck them in the waistband of his jeans. He set his tools inside the SUV and closed the tailgate. "It won't take long to rebuild. I'll get my brothers out here to help me tomorrow morning. With five of us working, we can get it done in a couple of hours."

She waited while he shrugged on the sheepskin-lined jacket he had abandoned earlier, when it got too hot. "Is Laramie always like this? Everyone helping everyone else? Or is that just because it's Christmas?"

Kevin accepted the mug and two frosted sugar cookies she gave him. The cocoa was hot and delicious. "I think Christmas inspires everyone to be generous, but Laramie is a great place year-round. People here take care of each other." It was why he had come back. Why he intended to stay.

Noelle took a sip of her own cocoa. "I've never seen anything quite like it."

"You being a big-city girl and all," he teased. Deciding to make himself comfortable, he settled his weight on the rear bumper.

Noelle sighed wistfully and sat down next to

him. "Houston has its perks, but a small town feel is not one of them."

They sipped the cocoa in silence, enjoying the starlit winter night. "Mikey asleep?" Kevin asked eventually.

"Yes." She rolled her eyes in maternal exasperation. "*Finally.* It took four more stories than usual to get him relaxed enough to be put down. He gets hyper, rather than sleepy, when he's overtired."

"Or in other words," Kevin guessed, chuckling, "once that second wind kicks in…"

She drew a deep breath. "Watch out."

They exchanged understanding smiles. "Do you have to work tomorrow?" she asked after a few moments of companionable silence.

Aware this was beginning to feel like a date, Kevin shook his head. "Nope. I'm off Saturday and Sunday this week."

She continued gazing at him.

"What?" he asked.

Noelle stood and faced him once again. "You look so different in these clothes versus your sheriff's department uniform," she explained finally.

"More disreputable?" he teased.

She let his joke pass without comment. "I didn't think detectives wore uniforms."

Surprised to find he wasn't the least bit tired despite the long day he'd had, Kevin stretched his legs out in front of him. "That's true in the big city. In low-crime places like Laramie, detectives do double duty—take patrol as well as answer calls for assistance."

"What other cases are you working on now?"

"Well, let's see." Kevin drew out the suspense while he munched one of the cookies she had given him. "Yesterday, there was the case of the missing leaf blower," he reported with exaggerated seriousness. "Turned out to be in the caller's backyard. He'd just forgotten to bring it in, and panicked when he didn't see it in his garage."

Noelle giggled. Kevin found it was all the encouragement he needed.

"Then there was the catnapping a couple of weeks ago. Turned out 'Tomcat' had a couple lady friends in heat. He returned home when that excitement ended. And let's not forget the case of the missing street signs from Hickory and Main. That remains unsolved, although I suspect the signs are in the custody of one or two of the town's teenagers and will be returned as soon as their parents stumble on them."

A mixture of amusement and respect sparkled in her eyes. "That all sounds…"

"Pedestrian? I guess it is. But compared to things I saw when I worked on the Houston police force," he said in all seriousness, "let's just say I prefer small town problems."

"And small town women?" Noelle asked. "Do you prefer them, too?"

Chapter Five

Noelle wanted to take the words back the moment they were out of her mouth, but now that she had spoken them, Kevin was clearly intrigued.

"Now why," he drawled, stepping closer, "would you want to know a thing like that?"

"I have no idea." Heart pounding, Noelle stepped back. It wasn't like her to be so reckless! "In fact, now that I think about it, the question was downright rude...so feel free to ignore it." She gathered up the empty mugs and the tray and hurried off.

He caught up with her in three long strides, clamped a hand on her shoulder and pivoted her around to face him. The outdoor lights bathed them in a soft glow. "Actually, I think I would like to answer that," he replied.

Noelle hitched in a breath.

He held her gaze deliberately. "I like women who tell the truth."

That was a warning volley if she had ever heard one.

"Especially beautiful women with soft lips and intelligent blue eyes. Women who know how to put a party together."

She couldn't help it—she laughed. "Now you're pulling my leg."

"Wrong again." He took the tray from her and set it in the grass. "I am very attracted to you. Just as you are very attracted to me."

She clamped her arms in front of her like a shield. "If that's the case, what's holding you back?"

Kevin propped his hands on his hips and frowned. "The combination of wariness and challenge I see in your eyes right now."

"Can you blame me?" Unwilling to think what it would be like if Kevin decided he wanted to thoroughly investigate every aspect of her life, she drew an unsteady breath. "I know you don't trust me," she finished.

"I'm a cop," he reminded her, his golden-brown brows drawing together. "I've seen the very best and the very worst of human nature. I don't trust anyone until they prove to me that I can trust them." He paused, still looking her up and down, from the top of her breeze-mussed hair to the toes of her leather boots and back again. "You don't seem all that surprised."

Noelle shrugged, wishing she didn't want so very much to kiss him again. "A part of me is very cynical, too."

"Any particular reason why?"

Knowing self-preservation was key, Noelle revealed as little as possible. "The usual," she said offhandedly. "I was betrayed by someone close to me and the experience was very disheartening, to say the least. I had a hard time bouncing back from the disillusionment."

"But you did bounce back," he noted softly, with something akin to admiration.

Noelle nodded, more than willing to share the lesson she'd learned. "Thanks to people like Dash and Miss Sadie and my late husband, Michael, and others I've come to know and trust. There are good people in the world, Kevin. And it's okay to let yourself open up and get close to them."

He continued to regard her thoughtfully. "People like you?"

Noelle broke eye contact. As always, when Kevin got near her like this, she felt her defenses come up. "I was speaking in generalities," she said stiffly.

"Now," he pointed out, closing the distance between them in two easy strides. "Earlier you were opening the door rather specifically."

Her palms flattened across his chest, holding him at bay. She had the strong suspicion he was thinking about kissing her again. "That was an impulse."

"And a good one." Kevin wrapped his arms around her. He grinned seductively. "Just like this…"

Noelle struggled to keep her feelings in check, but it was an impossible task when he was holding her flush against him. The turmoil inside her increased exponentially as his lips parted hers. He moved closer still and her skin registered the heat, the hardness of his body compared to hers. Their kiss deepened, their warm breaths blending. And this time she made no attempt to put on the brakes or pull away. She felt the pounding of his heart, the depth of his desire; she tasted the essence that was him. Over and over his tongue plunged into her mouth, stroking and arousing, making her aware of needs that until now she'd had no idea existed. She melted against him, wreathing her arms about his neck, completely caught up in the passionate mating of their lips and tongues. He made her feel like living again, in a way she'd never experienced.

His previous kiss had been experimental. This one was tender and giving, unlike anything she had ever felt before. And that somehow made the culmination of the desire that had been building between them all the sweeter.

Noelle had feared Kevin was the kind of man her father had been, that despite his charm and easy-going manner he was at heart guarded, cynical, unable to open up enough to give and receive love. As Kevin continued kissing and holding her, she saw that she was wrong. He wasn't just good with her son and willing to help others, he was a passionate and affectionate man, too.

Knowing just how potent the attraction between them was, Kevin hadn't intended to let their feelings take over. Hadn't intended to take her into his arms and kiss her again, the complications of their situation be damned. Nor had he wanted to allow himself to get any closer to Noelle. He had told himself to put the chemistry flowing between them on the back burner until his investigation was complete, her innocence verified, her secrets—whatever they were— revealed. But remaining emotionally aloof from her was proving to be a futile task. The more time he spent with her, the more he was drawn to her. He wanted to forget he was a cop, forget everything, just take her to bed and make wild, passionate love to her, so thoroughly and completely, neither of them would ever forget a single instant of it. He wanted to explore their attraction to each other, and worry about everything else later. Much later. He wanted to know what it would be like to be her lover, to go to sleep with her wrapped in his arms every night and wake up with her every morning.

He could tell by her response that she wanted this kind of emotional connection every bit as much as he did. To get involved, they'd have to put their hearts on the line. Which was, Kevin realized as he slowly let the kiss come to a close, exactly what they were doing.

Aware that he had never wanted to possess a woman more, he lifted his head and looked into her eyes. He'd expected them to be misty with passion, so the sparks of fury glimmering in them caught him by surprise.

"You just have to push the limits, don't you?" she said.

Kevin let her go as swiftly as if she had burned him. "Is that what you think I'm doing?" he asked. If so, he had to correct that misimpression, pronto.

Noelle chose her words carefully. "I think it's Christmas," she said. "And Christmas is a lonely time for people who aren't romantically involved. I think people in our situation sometimes do foolish things this time of year, only to look back come January and wonder what in the world they were thinking. I don't want this to be something either of us regrets."

She was correct—to a point. "I've had plenty of Christmases where I haven't been seeing anyone special and I've survived," he told her gruffly.

"So in other words—" she knelt to retrieve the tray and mugs he'd set in the grass earlier "—you're not hitting on me just to find someone of the opposite sex to take to family gatherings and exchange gifts with."

"Right. Although..." Kevin fell into step beside her as she headed for the front porch "...if you'd like to exchange gifts with me..."

She paused, then made a comical face. "We're already exchanging favors. My decorating the community center in exchange for you rebuilding the steps."

Kevin had never been happier about swapping chores with someone. "Your point being?"

Noelle paused at the door in a way that let him know he was not going to be asked back inside.

Her eyes took on a sober light. "Too much too soon is usually not a good thing. Especially when it comes to emotional entanglements."

Determined to end the evening on a more carefree note, Kevin teased, "What about just physical ones then?"

She took the comment in the joshing manner it was delivered. "I don't do just physical ones."

Good to know, Kevin thought, filing away that tidbit of information. "So no merry widow routine with you?" he ascertained with a great deal more satisfaction than was warranted.

"No," she said, frowning. "What about you? Are you in the habit of indiscriminately spreading *your* affections around?"

"I don't take a woman to bed," he told her honestly, "unless I can see myself building a future with her."

A playful smile tilted the corners of her lips. "I gather that doesn't happen often," she quipped wryly.

Kevin shoved a hand through his hair. "Let's just say my family thinks I'm a mite bit choosey."

She laughed softly, confessing, "I've heard pretty much the same thing from my friends."

"Including Dash Nelson?" Kevin asked.

"Dash doesn't want to date around any more than I do. He prefers the dinner-with-friends routine."

I'll bet.

"Speaking of which…" Noelle paused, "Dash asked me to go out with him tomorrow evening, to have dinner and discuss the progress of the holiday parties for Miss Sadie. I told him I would if I could find a sitter." Noelle regarded him hopefully. "Do you know anyone who might be interested?"

"Yes," Kevin said, taking opportunity where and when he found it. "Me."

"LET ME GET THIS STRAIGHT," Brad said on Saturday morning, as Kevin and his four brothers worked on rebuilding the side staircase at Blackberry Hill. "Another guy is taking the woman you're interested in out for dinner, and you're babysitting her son."

Will looked at Kevin as if he had lost his mind. And maybe he had, Kevin allowed. He hammered a board in place with four hard whacks, glad Noelle had taken Mikey into town to mail a stack of party invitations at the Laramie post office, thereby giving him this chance to speak frankly with his brothers. "That pretty much sums it up."

"Why would you ever volunteer for that?" Riley picked up another board and fitted it in place.

That was something Kevin had been trying to figure out since his unprecedented offer the previous evening. It wasn't like him to act first and think later—except when he was around Noelle. Then his male instincts seemed to take over, damn the consequences. Welcoming his siblings' outspoken take on the situation, Kevin cleared his throat. "To check out the competition?"

"Or play chaperone," Lewis guessed.

Kevin waited while Brad and Lewis measured and cut another two-by-six plank. "Okay. It might have occurred to me to play the spoiler in tonight's festivities."

"How?" Will smoothed off the edges of the cut wood with a power sander.

"I'm not sure exactly." The tool belt about his waist jangling, Kevin took the finished board and set it in place. "But I'm fairly certain I can dampen the mood. Or at least see where things seem to be headed by observing Dash and Noelle when they arrive home at the end of the evening."

Riley grinned. "Thereby discovering if you have any real competition or not."

Kevin held the board while Riley hammered his side in. "She says they're just friends."

"What does your competition think?" Brad asked as he measured off another piece of wood.

Kevin scowled. "Dash takes her for granted in a way that suggests he thinks the battle for her heart was fought and won a long time ago."

"You seem conflicted," Will noted.

Kevin shrugged. "I don't want to move in on another guy's territory if he's already staked a claim. That wouldn't be right. But if the woman doesn't agree the territory has been staked, then is it even an issue?"

"Seems to me the field is wide-open," Lewis said.

The rest of Kevin's brothers agreed.

So all he had to do, Kevin realized, was make the most of the opportunity given.

Not quite as simple as it sounded, he realized several hours later, when he arrived at Blackberry Hill, freshly showered and shaved, and encountered Noelle. She looked gorgeous in a red velvet dress, and Dash was at her side in a suit and tie. Was this the kind of guy she really wanted?

"Mikey's already asleep for the evening," she told Kevin with her usual cheerful efficiency. "He was so tired I had to put him down at six-thirty. He should sleep straight through. But if he wakes up and becomes distressed, you can call me on my cell and I'll come right home."

Had Dash Nelson looked the least bit unhappy about that, Kevin could have faulted him. Unfortunately, he seemed fine with it. Another point in his favor.

"Probably shouldn't stay out too late," Kevin remarked as they put their coats on and he shrugged out of his. "There's a cold front headed this way that might drop some freezing rain."

Dash frowned. "I thought that was supposed to stay northwest of us," he said.

Kevin shook his head. "The weather bureau has issued an advisory that includes Laramie County."

Now Dash did look annoyed.

"We'll hurry back," Noelle said, crushing Kevin's hope they might cancel their date and decide to stay in—with him as their guest, of course.

The two exited with barely a backward glance.

Feeling more dejected than he knew he had any right to be, Kevin opened up the armoire in the living room and sat down to watch television. Miss Sadie had satellite, so he was able to get a college bowl game. Normally, the football action would have interested him. Instead, all he could think about was the woman he wanted, sitting across the table from another man. Kevin slouched down on the sofa. So much for a holly jolly Christmas, he thought. "Bah, humbug," he muttered.

WHAT WAS WRONG WITH HER? Noelle wondered. Dash had taken her to a lovely country inn. A fire burned in the stone fireplace in the cozy dining room. There was plenty of fresh greenery and holly, and a beautifully decorated tree. Christmas music played softly in the background. Even the menu had a yuletide theme. Besides all that, Dash was as charming and chivalrous as ever. So why wasn't she enjoying herself? And, more importantly still, why did she feel that she would have been happier back at Miss Sadie's, with Mikey and Kevin McCabe?

"Something wrong with your turkey and cornbread stuffing?" Dash asked. "Because my roast beef and Yorkshire pudding was excellent. So if you'd rather have that…"

"No. The food's wonderful. Thank you. I'm just not as hungry as I thought. I'll take it home with me and enjoy it tomorrow."

"Dessert? Coffee?"

Noelle forced a smile. "No, thank you. I'd—"

Her words were cut short when the inn's front door opened and closed on a gust of bitterly cold wind. A dripping wet Rio Vasquez walked in and said something to the hostess. After a brief exchange, he strode on into the dining room.

"Sorry to interrupt your evening, folks. But the roads are getting bad, fast. The sheriff's department is asking everyone to get where they are going as soon as possible."

The proprietress added, "We have one room available with a four-poster bed for anyone who would like to stay."

Briefly, Dash looked hopeful. "If you'd rather not risk it, we could stay here tonight. That is, if you don't mind sharing."

Noelle had been pals with Dash forever. She couldn't fathom sharing a bed. "You've got all-wheel drive on your car, don't you?" she asked.

He nodded.

"Then I'm sure we'll be fine."

His face expressionless, Dash signaled the waiter. "I'll get our check." Short minutes later, they stepped outside, to find an icy rain coming down. "Good thing we don't have far to go," Dash said.

Noelle concurred. She soon realized law enforcement was right to get everyone off the roads as soon as possible. They were slick and treacherous. By the time she and Dash arrived at

Blackberry Hill and parked behind Kevin's aging SUV, her nerves were raw. She couldn't get inside soon enough.

Kevin was right where they had left him, parked on the sofa in front of the television, with the baby monitor beside him. While they shrugged out of their wet coats, he looked as relaxed as could be. "Home already, kids?" he quipped.

Shivering, Noelle came farther into the room. "The roads are really bad." She moved to stand next to the fire. "I don't think you should try and drive all the way back to Laramie. I think you should stay the night." She looked at Dash for confirmation. To her relief, he jumped in to agree.

"There are plenty of guest rooms upstairs. You can have your pick," Dash told Kevin graciously. "Although you might have to put linens on the bed."

"I'll take care of that," Noelle said. Exhausted from an evening spent trying to pay attention to Dash, when all she could really think about was Kevin, she carried the uneaten portion of her dinner into the kitchen and slid the white take-out box in the refrigerator, then returned. "I'll leave a light on in the room I make up for you, Kevin. Then if you all don't mind, I'm going to go ahead and turn in. Mikey will be up early."

Kevin looked disappointed that she was ducking out on them. Dash was focused on the football game. "Sleep well," Kevin told her with a gentle smile.

"See you in the morning," Dash added.

Noelle headed for the stairs, relieved.

"WANT A BEER?" Dash turned to Kevin affably after Noelle left.

Figuring this was as good a time as any to get to know his competition, and maybe figure out what it was Noelle saw in him, Kevin nodded. "Sure."

Dash walked to the kitchen and returned with two imported beers and a bowl of popcorn. "Not exactly the evening you had planned, hmm?" Kevin said, unable to help himself. For reasons he preferred not to examine too closely, he needed to know what Dash's intentions toward Noelle were.

"No kidding." The attorney lifted the beer to his lips, then paused, scowling at the action on screen. "I was expecting to lay the groundwork this evening."

"For?"

Dash slanted him a confident look. "Noelle doesn't know it, but I'm going to propose to her on Christmas Eve, during the open house Aunt Sadie and I are hosting here at Blackberry Hill. I've already ordered the ring."

"It's that serious?"

"It will be," he predicted, "as soon as she says yes."

"I guess you two have known each other awhile," Kevin said finally, telling himself it wasn't over till it was over.

"We met eight years ago. We've only started to get really close in the last year or so."

Kevin ignored the knot in his gut. "You've been in love with her all that time?" he probed.

Dash's expression turned rueful. "It shows, huh?"

Kevin nodded. Not that Noelle had seemed to notice… Either that or she was very good at keeping a poker face.

"Listen, I've got a favor to ask you," Dash said,

as an updated weather advisory flashed across the television screen. "My aunt Sadie wants the outside decorations up as soon as possible, and a big tree in here as well. Do you know anyone I could hire to help Noelle with that, say, by tomorrow afternoon, if the roads clear? I'd do it myself, but I've got this case going back in Houston, and I've got to be in court again first thing Monday morning."

"No problem," Kevin said smoothly. "I'll take care of it."

"Thanks, man. I knew I could count on you."

Maybe to steal your woman, Kevin thought, as both men headed up to bed. Although in all fairness the only person who thought Noelle was Dash's woman was Dash. What mattered was what Noelle felt. And she did not appear to be in lust—or in love—with her old buddy. That didn't mean, however, that she wouldn't say yes to his proposal. People married for all sorts of reasons. Convenience. Security. To provide a father for their child.

For someone like Noelle, who, according to

public records, no longer had a family of her own, what Miss Sadie and Dash were offering might be just the ticket she had been waiting for. Then again, it might not be enough. She might want the full package—love, companionship, passion, friendship—as much as Kevin did. Noelle certainly hadn't appeared to voluntarily settle for less thus far. In the meantime, he groused, as he took off his boots and stretched out on the freshly made-up bed, he had turned into the world's biggest worrier.

Oh, he might have played it cool when Dash and Noelle walked in this evening, but his stomach had been tied in knots the whole time they'd been gone. First, he'd been concerned there was something brewing between Dash and Noelle after all, or soon would be. Then he'd been apprehensive about the icy rain and increasingly bad roads. Now, he was fearful that Dash would make his move on Noelle before Kevin had a chance to solve this case and bring his intentions toward Noelle out in the open. Whether he could compete with eight years of an enduring friendship between Noelle and Dash was another question altogether.

The last thing Kevin wanted to do was fall for a woman who was halfway interested in another man. Yet if he let Dash make his move, without first seeing where this attraction between himself and Noelle could lead, he'd spend the rest of his life wondering what might have happened if only he'd dare pursue her.

SHE COULDN'T SLEEP. And Noelle knew why. Throwing back the covers on her bed, she rose, put on her slippers and headed quietly toward the stairs.

She was in the midst of preparing hot cocoa in the kitchen when footsteps sounded behind her. She turned to see Kevin framed in the doorway. His hair was rumpled and feet clad only in warm thermal socks. Otherwise, he was dressed as he had been earlier that evening, in a corduroy shirt and jeans. Just like before, merely looking at him stirred her senses. His dark eyes gentled even as his lips curved in a sexy half smile.

"Everything okay?" he asked.

Noelle shrugged her shoulders and went back to looking for the vanilla extract. "Why wouldn't it be?"

"I don't know." Kevin lounged against the counter next to the stove. "Maybe because it's two in the morning and you're down here making cocoa instead of sound asleep upstairs."

Wishing she had thought to put on a robe—or at least a bra—beneath her flannel pajamas before heading downstairs, Noelle measured out cocoa powder, sugar, vanilla and a dash of salt, then added them to the pan. "I couldn't sleep."

His glance drifted over her body in a frank, sensual appraisal before returning to her face. "Any particular reason why not?"

More conscious of him than of what she was making, Noelle whisked the ingredients with a practiced touch. "Stress. Christmas is only days away, and I've got way too much to do."

"If it will make you feel any better, I've already promised Dash I would spend tomorrow helping you with the outdoor decorations."

Finding his low, husky voice a bit too full of

erotic promise for comfort, Noelle turned away. "How did that come about?" she asked, rummaging through the cabinet for marshmallows.

"Same way as the steps." Seeing she couldn't reach them, Kevin stepped in to get the marshmallows for her. "Dash was looking for assistance, and I volunteered my services."

Their fingertips brushed as he handed her the package. Aware that the brief contact had caused her nipples to tighten and her pulse to kick up another notch, Noelle smiled. "You do that a lot."

He folded his arms over the hard muscles of his chest. "'Tis the season…"

"Meaning what?" Noelle carefully poured hot cocoa into mugs and topped them with miniature marshmallows. "Come New Year's it will be back to every man for himself."

"Probably not." Once they sat down at the kitchen table, he sipped his cocoa. When their gazes met, there was a moment of sizzling sexual tension. "I seem to volunteer a lot."

Forcing back her turbulent emotions, Noelle mused, "So do I, actually."

"Does that make us chumps?" he asked, a hint of approval in his eyes. Contemplating the notion, he ran a hand beneath his jaw, his fingers caressing the stubble that made him look even more ruggedly handsome than usual.

"Or just naturally generous individuals," she replied, finding herself growing distracted by her wayward thoughts.

She didn't know what it was—the coziness of the kitchen, the late hour or the intimacy of the conversation—but she could feel herself gravitating toward him. Although she knew getting involved with Kevin McCabe would put her hard-won serenity on the line, she couldn't deny that the way he was looking at her made her feel more gloriously alive than she had in months. "I think I prefer the latter."

"Me, too." Their eyes met and held for another breath-stealing moment. Kevin nodded at the yellow notepad and pen on the center of the table. "So what's on your list?" he asked casually.

"The list contains all the things I have yet to do for Miss Sadie's two parties—the open house for two hundred people on Christmas Eve, and the sit-down dinner for twenty folks on Christmas Day. Both events are going to be catered, but there is still so much to do to pull all the details together. In addition to that, there are all the things I want to do for myself and Mikey this year."

"Like what?" Kevin asked.

"I promised him he could see Santa Claus. I wanted to take him around one evening and show him all the holiday lights and decorations. He needs to see the nativity scene at the church at night. And I planned to take him out caroling one evening, with a group of people. I also thought it would be fun for him to see snow."

"That's a pretty ambitious agenda," Kevin noted admiringly, taking her hand in his.

Noelle savored the warmth of his touch. "I want to make up for all I didn't do for him in terms of celebrating the holiday the past two years. I want to feel Christmas again, in my heart. And I want him to feel it, too."

Kevin's fingers tightened around hers. "Seems to me you've made a good start."

"Thanks." Noelle withdrew her hand and sat back with a frown. "But I don't see how I'm going to make good on all the promises I've made to him."

"You could always ask Dash to find someone to take over for you, and concentrate on your son," Kevin suggested.

"I can't do that." She wanted him to understand the root of her devotion. "I owe Dash and Miss Sadie so much. More than I can ever repay them. Dash took me on pro bono and helped me sort out all the legal stuff after my parents died. I don't know what I would have done at that time if he hadn't been there for me. And Miss Sadie took me under her wing when I was just nineteen. She convinced me my talents were being wasted as a banquet server, and got me a job as an event planner instead."

Kevin stretched his legs out beneath the table, his leg briefly brushing hers. "I'm surprised you didn't go to college."

Aware they were headed into dangerous personal territory, Noelle traced the smooth surface of the mug with her thumb. "I wanted to but it wasn't possible."

His brow furrowed. "You mean financially?"

She avoided his eyes and stated simply, "I was an emotional wreck after my parents died."

He reached over and took her hand again, offering wordless comfort.

Trying hard not to give in to the compassion flowing from him, for fear she would end up in his arms again, Noelle took a deep breath. "I just didn't have the focus needed to attend classes, and then I started working and got my education and training on the job, so college wasn't necessary. I'm making a good living without it."

He seemed to know she was leaving out as much as she was telling him. "But you like what you do?"

"Oh, yes." Noelle was relieved to be able to say that sincerely. "Especially the last few years, since I went into business for myself and have been able to pick and choose what jobs I want to take, and tailor my hours to fit Mikey's schedule." Growing anxious over having to mentally censor what she said about her past, she stood up and carried her mug to the sink. "For instance, had Miss Sadie not fallen and broken her leg, I'd be taking two weeks off right now. There's no way I could do that if I was working for someone else." She chattered on, rinsing out the mug. "Not at one of the busiest times of the year for event planners. And speaking of busy…what about those side steps? We need them in working order by the time of the party. Can you still paint them tomorrow?"

Kevin stood, too. The reserve was back in his eyes, along with the lingering desire. "The wood has to dry out before we can apply primer and paint." He held up a staying hand before she could protest. "Don't worry. I'll have it done in time for Christmas. In the meanwhile," he continued, "I'll help you and Mikey out in any way I can."

Chapter Six

"Can you believe this weather?" Dash asked cheerfully, early the next morning.

Kevin cast a glance at the sun streaming in through Miss Sadie's kitchen windows. "You'd never know there was freezing rain last night," he murmured, looking outside. One would never know that he and Noelle had enjoyed a very informative chat just hours before, in this very room, either. Or guess, from her confident manner now, that whenever the subject of her background or past came up she turned into a bundle of nerves.

Kevin couldn't shake the feeling that Noelle needed him to rescue her every bit as much as the kids who had been picked on in school had. He knew that whatever was forcing her to keep her guard up was not going to go away until she had dealt with it. It was just a hunch, but he felt as if he had been sent there to help her deal with it. Now all he had to do was get her to trust him enough to let him assist her....

Noelle took a look at the glistening puddles on the new wooden staircase at the side door. "Except for the fact it's wet outside," she agreed.

"Even the moisture will be all dried up in a few hours," Dash said, helping Mikey find a Cheerio he had dropped on his lap.

Grinning, the toddler picked it up and shoved it into his mouth. "More!" he said, pounding his high chair tray.

"More, please," Noelle corrected.

Mikey grinned, parroting in the same soft sing-song voice as his mother, "More. Please."

Ruffling his hair in approval, Noelle spread another fistful in front of him. She turned to Kevin. "Can I get you some coffee? Breakfast?"

How about a kiss instead? he thought, but nodded. "Whatever you've got would be great."

"Well, sad to say, I have to hit the road." Dash

stood and shrugged on his coat. "I've got to get back to the office to prepare for trial tomorrow." He walked over to accept the travel mug of coffee from Noelle. "I'm going to be really busy, so you may not hear from me for a few days, but I'll see you next weekend."

Noelle smiled and returned his casual hug goodbye. "Good luck with the case."

"Thanks." Dash shook Kevin's hand, bent to press a kiss to the top of Mikey's head, and let himself out the door.

Noelle slid a plate of some sort of breakfast casserole, fruit and toast in front of Kevin. "Change your mind about helping me today?" she asked.

He dug into the food enthusiastically. "No way. I'm here for the duration," he vowed.

Noelle beamed. "Then eat up. 'Cause I plan to run us both ragged." She winked at her son. "Right, Mikey?"

Mikey giggled and pounded his tray. "Right!"

NOELLE HADN'T BEEN kidding, Kevin thought some eight hours later. She'd had him up on a ladder stringing lights across the front of the house, while she and Mikey put electric candles and evergreen wreaths in every window. He'd then hauled additional wire-mounted light displays of Santa's sleigh and reindeer, along with plastic candy canes and a directional sign to the North Pole, from the basement storeroom up to the rolling front lawn. None of the decorations had been used for several years. They were all dusty, and in some cases, covered with cobwebs. Cleaning them up was a tedious but necessary job. Trying to arrange them to Noelle's satisfaction, even worse.

"I just don't know what we're going to do with those candy canes," Noelle complained, after Kevin had situated them for the sixth time. Holding Mikey on her hip, she moved around to study them from another angle. "They are so faded."

Actually, Kevin noted, the candy canes were bordering on tacky. Unlike the rest of the decorations, which would add a touch of class.

"But Miss Sadie told me she wanted me to use them," Noelle continued pensively.

"I think I recall being held at the business end of one," Kevin drawled facetiously. "I just didn't know it had been per Miss Sadie's instruction."

Remembering the first day they had met, Noelle whirled to face him. "Very funny." She wrinkled her nose. "For your information, Miss Sadie had nothing to do with my use of the candy cane as a weapon. Only I can take credit for that comedy of errors."

"Good to know," Kevin quipped. They both chuckled. The playful moment suddenly turned heated, and he could have sworn Noelle was thinking about kissing him again. He was not surprised. He was thinking the same thing…and had been all day.

Blushing fiercely, she turned away and concentrated on positioning the candy canes. "Miss Sadie has used these on either side of the front door for the last twenty years, whenever she was in Laramie at Christmastime." Noelle shifted Mikey to her other hip. "They have huge sentimental value, so I guess we could paint them." Mikey was getting squirmy, so she set him down on the lawn. "Do you think that could work?"

"Probably. As long as you properly primed and sealed them."

She stepped back to regard the progress thus far, watching as Mikey toddled over to cautiously inspect the Santa Claus. "For every little job we take on, we create ten more big jobs, it seems."

Deciding a friendly hug was in order, Kevin wrapped his arm about her shoulders. "And Merry Christmas to you, too," he murmured in her ear.

"I mean it." Noelle tipped her head up. "I feel so overwhelmed," she whispered.

Kevin smiled down at her. "Also a tradition at Christmas."

She studied him. "You are not going to let me throw myself a pity party, are you?"

"Not this time of year, no. Haven't you heard?" He gave her another reassuring squeeze. "It's the happiest time of the year."

Noelle giggled. "Okay, now you've got me smiling again."

"Good." Kevin knelt and held out his arms. The

two-year-old ran over and climbed up into them. "Mikey and I like you that way."

Noelle sighed. "It doesn't mean that I feel any less overwhelmed."

Kevin shrugged, holding the cuddly toddler in his arms. "Only one cure for that. Get busy and finish, so we can cross more items off your list."

LATE THAT AFTERNOON, Kevin went home to shower and change into clothes suitable for painting. On the way back, he picked up the items Noelle needed from the hardware store.

"Get everything?" She met him at the back door with Mikey in her arms. She had never looked more beautiful than she did at that moment, burnished curls framing her oval face, cheeks ripe with color, eyes alight with purpose.

"Yep." Kevin couldn't get over what a welcoming sight the two of them were. Or how happy he was to be here, just hanging out, doing chores with them. "Including the exact paint you asked for—candy-cane-red and snow-white." He took the spray primer out of one of the sacks. "Do you want to try and get these painted tonight?" he asked, pointing to the twin candy canes.

"How long does each coat take to dry?"

"Thirty minutes," he replied.

Noelle didn't have to think long. "Then, yes. Can you stay to help?"

He had been hoping she would ask. "Sure."

She flashed him a sexy smile. "Can you also stay for dinner?"

Kevin rubbed his jaw in a parody of thoughtfulness, even though he already knew what his answer was going to be. "What are we having?"

"Mikey's favorites. Fish sticks, mac'n'cheese, green beans and applesauce."

"G'een beans!" Mikey shouted.

"What do you know." Kevin picked up the candy canes and primer, ready to head toward the door. "My favorites, too."

Noelle mocked him with her eyes. "I'm sure you eat a lot of fish sticks."

Kevin winked. "If I were hanging around you, I might."

She grinned, knowing the truth of that.

Twenty minutes later he'd finished priming and was washing his hands in the utility sink.

"Want to hang on to Mikey while I put supper on the table?" Noelle asked.

"My pleasure." Kevin hoisted the child in his arms.

While she bustled about the kitchen, he lounged against the counter with Mikey cradled against his chest. Content with the view from up there, the little boy placed his hands on Kevin's cheeks and stared deep into his eyes. He moved his index finger to the middle of Kevin's face. "Nose."

"That's right," he exclaimed. "That's my nose."

"'hin." Mikey pointed again.

"Right again," Kevin declared, enjoying the game as much as his small cohort. "That's my chin."

Whirling toward them, Noelle sucked in a breath. "Watch your eyes," she cautioned.

"Too late." Kevin blinked, guiding to one side the small digit poking at his eyelashes.

"Honey, be careful," Noelle told Mikey gently.

He looked at Kevin solemnly. "Hon', be ca'ful."

Kevin burst out laughing.

Mikey chuckled, too.

Noelle shook her head.

Dinner, bath and storytime passed with the same jocularity. Kevin taught Mikey to pretend sleep and pretend snore while they cuddled on the sofa, a talent Mikey found hilarious and worthy of many giggles. Noelle joined in on the fun a few minutes later.

Was this what it would be like to spend the holidays with a wife and son? Kevin wondered, enjoying the loving, familial atmosphere. If so, he knew what he wanted for Christmas. It was right here with Noelle and Mikey.

Unfortunately, all good things had to come to an end, and soon it was time for Mikey to head to bed. "Say good night to Kevin," Noelle encouraged, nestling her son in her arms.

Mikey leaned forward to give him a hug. Instead of letting go, he wrapped his arms around Kevin's neck and tried to shift his weight to him. "Tuck!" he ordered.

Noelle's eyes widened in surprise. "He's asking you to tuck him in bed."

Kevin looked at her. "It's okay with me, if it's okay with you."

She shrugged, looking as pleased as he felt. "Sure. You can carry him up for me."

Noelle gathered up Mikey's blanket and two stuffed toys, then trailed after them up the stairs. She went into the room temporarily dubbed the nursery, and placed the items in the portable travel crib where he was sleeping. Hugs and kisses followed for Mikey—and his stuffed animals. Kevin slipped out first. Noelle joined him downstairs several minutes later, baby monitor in hand.

"He down for the night?" Kevin asked.

She made a comical face. "He's not asleep. But he's content. Sometimes he'll play for half an hour or so before he actually nods off. Especially when he's had such an exciting day—having you here with us."

Kevin nodded companionably. "Makes sense he'd have trouble winding down."

They heard Mikey talking softly to his animals, giggling as if in on a very private joke. "See what

I mean?" Noelle said, shaking her head in fond exasperation.

Aware they still had a lot to do, Kevin stood. "You want me to help you with the dishes or go ahead and get started painting the candy canes?"

She gave him an openly admiring glance. "You're really hanging in there."

"Hey." Kevin palmed his chest. "I'm like the Energizer bunny."

Her blue eyes sparkled. "Or is it the Energizer reindeer?"

Kevin pretended to think about it. "Elf, maybe?"

She took his elbow and half led, half pushed him toward the kitchen. "You're a little more than Santa's helper," she said appreciatively.

Sensing they were at a turning point in their relationship, Kevin faced her. "Yeah?" he challenged, wanting her to put whatever she was thinking and feeling into words. "What am I?" Suddenly, he wanted to know where he stood with her. Right here. Right now.

"Speaking bluntly?" she said softly. "The nicest man I've ever met."

BY THE TIME Noelle joined Kevin fifteen minutes later, he had all the white stripes painted on both candy canes and was wiping his hands on a rag. He looked sexy and at ease in a white T-shirt, soft gray sweatshirt and jeans. He trotted up the new staircase to her side. "I think we should wait for the first color to dry before adding the second, don't you?" he asked.

"I do." As she surveyed his handiwork, Kevin edged closer and the sleeve of his sweatshirt brushed her arm. "Otherwise it might smear."

Together, they turned and went inside the house. "I feel bad that I'm working you so hard," Noelle confided. Guiltier still about the way she was lusting after him. She wasn't used to feeling the intense physical longing she experienced whenever she was around him.

Kevin washed his hands in the utility sink, then turned to her with a grin. "I've got an idea."

Noelle hitched in a gulp of air.

"Got any of those iced sugar cookies left?"

Okay, so maybe they weren't on the same page,

sexually speaking. "Plenty." Aware that was exactly the same kind of request Dash would have hit her with in this situation, she forced her most efficient smile. "How about a mug of coffee to go with it?" No one could say she wasn't a gracious hostess.

"Perfect." Looking remarkably content, Kevin leaned against the counter while she filled the coffeemaker. "Dash doesn't know what he's missing."

Noelle ignored the frustration welling up inside her. Since when had she cared whether a man put the moves on her or not? It was ridiculous for her to feel hurt that Kevin McCabe hadn't tried to kiss her again, when all he was doing was respecting the parameters she had set out. She got out the cookie tin, opened the lid and offered it to Kevin. "I think he does. I think that's why he's hiding in his law office in Houston."

Kevin took out two cookies and munched contentedly. "Not much for physical labor, huh?"

Noelle left the open tin on the counter between them, in case Kevin wanted more. "I think Dash is more cerebral." The coffeemaker gurgled behind her as it neared the end of the brewing cycle. "Although he does love Mikey and vice versa."

"I noticed." Kevin paused. He gave her a bluntly assessing look. "He'd make a good dad."

Darned if he hadn't put her on the defensive already. Noelle lifted her shoulders in a reflective shrug. "Maybe. Someday. When Dash is ready to marry and have a family of his own," she allowed.

Kevin moved closer, the brisk woodsy scent of his cologne inundating them both. "I was talking about—"

Noelle held up a hand. "I know what you were talking about." And she didn't want to discuss it.

He lifted a curious brow. "Not gonna happen?"

My, he was perceptive. Avoiding his penetrating glance, Noelle set about pouring them each a mug of coffee. She got the cream and sugar out and set them on the table. "Never say never," she murmured, taking a seat and indicating he should do the same. "But...I'd have to be in love again to ever marry."

"And you're not?" Kevin pressed, settling next to her.

Noelle could see what he was getting at. "With Dash? No." She drew a deep breath. "What about you? Do you want to marry and have kids?"

"Yes. Very much." He leaned toward her. "But like you, I'm going to have to be in love. I would never say 'I do' to someone just to have a child."

"Me, either."

Kevin took a long drink of coffee and studied her contemplatively. "So what do you usually do in the evenings when Mikey is in bed?"

"Work on events I'm hired to plan." Noelle knew how dull that sounded, but it was the life she had chosen for herself since her husband died, and she had never really minded all the alone time—until now. "That's when I do all the menus and address invitations, compile RSVP lists and so on."

"Ah." He reached out and covered her hand with his own.

"It's hard to do too much of that when Mikey is awake unless I have a sitter, so I do as much of the prep work as I can while he's sleeping. I don't want to miss anything, you know? I guess I want to make every second count with Mikey, really be present in his life."

Kevin regarded her with understanding. "So what would you be doing right now if you could do anything you wanted?" he asked.

"Truthfully?" Noelle sighed wistfully. "I'd be kissing you again."

It wasn't until his eyes widened that she realized she had said the last words out loud. Noelle blushed and clapped a hand over her mouth in shock. Talk about a Freudian slip! It was one thing to be feeling so attracted to Kevin McCabe, another to let him know how much she wanted him.

"Good thing I've got this, then," Kevin drawled, reaching into his pants pocket.

Noelle's heart pounded at the mischief glimmering in his eyes. Her imagination ran wild... until she spied the sprig of greenery and small roll of tape.

"We deputies always like to come prepared for anything." Kevin stood and fastened the mistletoe to the kitchen door frame. "Now all we need," he continued in the same low, sexy tone as he took her hand and pulled her to her feet, "is some pretty lady to test it out." Drawing her near, he wrapped both hands around her waist and positioned her in the portal. "Might that be you, Ms. Kringle?"

She glanced at the mistletoe directly above her head. "It might," she teased back. It seemed she and Kevin McCabe were on the same page, after all. She regarded him with mock sternness. "Provided I'm properly persuaded."

He tilted his head to the side and lowered his lips to hers. "Then let's see what we can do about that," he whispered as their breaths meshed.

He held her mouth under his as he inundated her with slow kisses and the comfortable warmth of his tall, strong body. It had been three long years since she had let herself be loved, let herself feel. Maybe it was Christmas, Noelle thought, as his tongue swept into her mouth, searching out every tender, aching spot. Maybe it was his kindness that had her blood bubbling with pent-up desire. She kissed him back, moaning with pleasure as his hands slid sensuously through her hair, realizing she had never wanted anyone the way she desired Kevin McCabe. For the very first time in her life she was willing to let go of all her fears and live in the moment.

For too long she had been embittered by the past and the actions of those close to her. Maybe it was the spirit of Christmas seeping into her heart, maybe it was being in Laramie and experiencing firsthand how loving, generous and open the people here were. All Noelle knew for certain was that she had been searching for a place that felt like home for what seemed an eternity. And there was no safer harbor than Kevin McCabe's arms....

Buying the mistletoe at the hardware store, along with the paint, had been an impulse. A way to humorously open the door to a good-night kiss. Kevin hadn't expected it to go beyond that, but now that he felt her sweet surrender, he couldn't have been happier. Instinct told him that Noelle hadn't been well-loved in the past. He intended to change that.

Deepening the kiss, he turned her so she was flush against the wall. He moved his hands to her breasts, caressing and soothing first through her clothes, then beneath. His body hardened when her nipples pebbled against his palms. Aware they were on the brink of no return, and he was probably moving way too fast, he reluctantly broke off the kiss.

Trembling, Noelle buried her face in his shoulder, her arms still wreathed about his neck. He felt the first of her regrets even before she pushed away, readjusted her clothing and stepped back.

Kevin saw the confusion on her face and knew he had been right to stop. Even if it had darn near killed him to do so. "We have to talk about this," he told her.

"Maybe it would be best if we didn't," she said in a low, strangled voice.

"Because...?"

"You're going to want to know what this means," she declared anxiously, "and I don't *know* what it means."

Kevin did. It meant that, despite everything, he

was developing strong feelings for her. Professionally speaking, he probably should have stuck to his original plan and waited until his investigation into Miss Sadie's identity theft was complete. Instead, he had been hanging around here all weekend, and surrendered to temptation because his instincts were telling him that despite the suspicious way she sometimes behaved, he could trust Noelle. Deep down, he knew that Miss Sadie had nothing to fear, and everything to gain, from her long-standing association with this woman.

Noelle poured the rest of her coffee into the sink and stood, her back to him, gripping the edge of the counter with both hands. "I'm not usually led around by my…hormones."

He moved behind her. Hands on her shoulders, he turned her gently to face him. "That kiss was more than hormones and we both know it," Kevin said gruffly.

"Regardless…" Confusion turned her eyes a darker blue. "I can't just do whatever I feel like doing. I have a son to consider."

He caught her wrist when she tried to pass by

him. "You know I would never do anything to hurt you or Mikey."

"Maybe not deliberately." She scowled, her frustration with the situation apparent. "But if Mikey starts to depend on you, just a little bit, or look forward to seeing you every day and then suddenly you're not around, he will be hurt, Kevin."

Ignoring the way her breasts were rising and falling with every emotional breath she took, Kevin released his hold on her. "Are we talking about Mikey or you?"

Her soft lips took on a defiant curve. "As good as that felt…just now—" she started in a tone too casual to be believed.

Triumphant, Kevin interrupted, "So you admit there's something between us."

Ignoring his question, she began to pace the kitchen restlessly. "I thought I could live in the moment, Kevin."

He struggled to remain calm. "But?"

She whirled to face him. "Turns out, I don't want a holiday fling."

Kevin didn't, either. He didn't want to start

anything, only to have it end a few weeks later. Willing to give her breathing room, if that was what she needed, he lounged against the sink. "What if it's more than that?"

Noelle swallowed. "There's no way we can know that."

"Maybe not right now," he countered, flashing her a teasing grin. "After a few more days and nights like this I reckon we're going to have a pretty good idea where we're headed."

She regarded him in exasperation. "You're so confident."

"With good reason," Kevin told her softly, closing the distance between them once again. He touched the side of her face with the back of his hand. "And so should you be. We aren't kids, Noelle." He paused to search her eyes. "We've lived enough to know when something isn't all that special versus something that only comes along once in a great while—if we're lucky."

"You're a hard man to resist," Noelle admitted reluctantly.

He delivered another kiss, glad the conversation

was back on less contentious ground. "Just keep thinking that way," he murmured persuasively.

To Kevin's disappointment, Noelle refused to smile. Her soft lips remained clamped together in a worried line. "I can't guarantee I'll stop being afraid to risk the kind of involvement that you seem to want from me," she admitted.

He refused to be discouraged. "Just promise me you'll keep making time to see me."

"As a friend," she agreed at last.

Kevin looked her straight in the eye. "And potential lover."

Chapter Seven

Monday turned out to be a great day for Kevin. He got the break in the case he had been hoping for, and when he went to see Miss Sadie, Noelle and Mikey were with her. From the way Noelle looked at him when he walked in, he guessed she had been thinking about the kisses they had shared as much as he had.

The elderly woman was looking well, he was happy to see. After greeting her warmly, he bent to say hello to Mikey, who was sitting on the floor playing with a shape sorter. Then Kevin quickly brought Noelle and Sadie up to speed. "I just talked to the Houston Police Department. They arrested two women returning illegally ordered goods with a credit card receipt in your name,

Miss Sadie. The suspects admitted to selling other items, also purchased in your name, on one of the Internet auction sites. The D.A. has talked the women into cooperating. So far they've identified ten other people involved in the identity theft ring, all of whom have been arrested."

"So it's over?" Noelle asked in relief. "They've found the lowlifes who have been stealing from those twenty-five families?"

"Not quite." Kevin helped Mikey fit a triangle-shaped block in the corresponding slot, then handed him a round one and pointed to a circular opening. "We still don't know who masterminded the scam." Kevin patted Mikey on the head, then stood. "The thieves claimed they got all their instructions over the Internet from someone named The Wizard."

"The person who's been transmitting orders via a computer at the public library," Miss Sadie concluded.

Kevin nodded. "That's what we suspect."

Silence fell in the room. "How did they get connected with this criminal genius?" Noelle asked at last. When the shape sorter was filled, she helped her son empty it out again.

Kevin took a chair next to her. "Apparently, the thieves all had suffered big losses on an online gambling site, and the cyber bookie involved had threatened them and their families with bodily harm unless they agreed to start fencing the stolen merchandise and turning over the proceeds—in cash—to a bogus nonprofit, set up to save the Armenian cave beetle."

Noelle wrinkled her nose. "Who's in charge of the charity?"

"Nobody knows." Kevin shrugged. "It was operated out of an office in a building known for its low occupancy. According to some of the other tenants, no one ever actually moved into the space."

"It was just used as an address for mail collection."

"Right. The cops have the office—and the library—under surveillance, but the thieves had already been told the money drop and the procedure for fencing the goods was going to change, and to await further instructions, which are supposed to come via the Internet sometime today."

"And of course the Houston police are waiting for them," Noelle guessed, looking relieved rather than worried.

"Right."

"It sounds complicated," she mused.

"Very," Kevin agreed. He and the HPD detectives had spent all morning studying the cyber evidence and unraveling it via teleconferences between their two departments.

Miss Sadie spoke up. "How much money has been stolen?"

Kevin winked at Mikey, who beamed up at him. "If you include the gambling losses, close to five million dollars in just six weeks."

Both women looked shocked.

"Not to worry, Miss Sadie. We'll get all this cleared up shortly," he promised.

She smiled. "I'm not worried. I know how competent you are, Detective McCabe. Speaking of which," she continued slyly, "I hear you've been a great deal of help to Noelle and Mikey the last few days."

Kevin smiled good-naturedly at the compliment.

"My nephew, Dash, should take a page from your book, Detective," Sadie continued.

Noelle eyed her employer with barely checked amusement. "Dash has done plenty for me, Miss Sadie."

"Except marry you," the elderly woman countered.

"Miss Sadie!" she chided.

Sadie lifted a hand. "I know, I know. We've been over this."

"Is there something I should know?" Kevin asked, wondering how much Miss Sadie knew about her nephew's plans, if anything.

"Like what?" Noelle demanded, shooting an annoyed glare his way.

Kevin couldn't pass up the chance to test the waters. "An engagement in the offing?" he said innocently.

"No!" Noelle declared.

At the same time Miss Sadie muttered, "One can hope!"

Noelle arched a brow. "I don't want to get married again any more than you do, Miss Sadie."

"Our situations are not the same at all," she retorted.

"Sure they are." Noelle stood and began gathering up her belongings and stuffed them into a carryall. "We both loved our husbands. We've both been there, done that."

"With one slight difference," Sadie corrected with obvious affection. "I'm eighty-five and I was married for sixty-three years. You're twenty-seven and—unlike me—still have a great deal of living ahead of you. You need to give love another chance, Noelle. If not with Dash, then with someone else."

"SOUNDS LIKE MISS SADIE has your life all charted out for you," Kevin remarked as he walked Noelle out to the parking lot, toting Mikey in his arms. He was glad that last night he had nailed down a time to help her pick out a Christmas tree for the Blackberry Hill living room and truck it out there. Otherwise, he had the feeling Noelle would have found some other way to get the job done, without him.

She paused as they stepped out into the winter sunshine, and rummaged through her purse. "She's very sweet. She just thinks all women my age are better off married."

"And you don't?" Kevin threw down the gauntlet, knowing Noelle would pick it right back up and brandish it at him.

Finally finding her keys, Noelle extracted them from her bag and zipped it closed. "I think," she said, as Mikey reached over and patted her head, "fate often gives you something quite different than what you want or expect, and when that happens you have to deal with it."

"Here we go again." Kevin extricated Mikey's fingers from his mother's curls. "Talking cryptically."

Noelle made a face at him. "Or philosophically."

"Seriously." Kevin took his time walking across the pavement to her van. "Wouldn't you want to be married again?" he asked casually, as Mikey studied the landscape over his shoulder.

"It's complicated," Noelle muttered.

At last, a chink in her emotional armor. "Complicated how?" Kevin pressed.

A distant look came into her eyes. "I come with my own set of baggage."

"Don't we all," he countered dryly.

"I don't think I want to burden anyone else with the problems of my past."

"I can't imagine anything where you're concerned being too tough to tackle," he observed.

The haunted look was back in her blue eyes. "Then you can't conjure up much, can you?" she quipped, morphing into the wisecracker she became whenever she felt at all threatened.

Aware they had some very important boundaries to set, Kevin shifted Mikey to his other arm. "Are you playing hard to get?" He leaned close enough to inhale her lavender perfume. "'Cause I have to tell you—it's not working at all in discouraging me."

A sexy grin spread across her face. "I *am* hard to get."

"So I'm finding out." Kevin kept his eyes on

hers, even as he prevented the mischievous little boy from taking off his deputy hat and tossing it to the wind.

"Make that *impossible* to get." Noelle continued the repartee as they reached her van.

With Mikey still cradled against his chest, Kevin leaned against the driver's door while she opened the sliding door at the back. "Dash Nelson doesn't think so."

Noelle let out a dramatic sigh. "Do I hear a hint of the competitive spirit in there?"

He quirked a brow. "Is it a race?" If so, he knew who was going to win. Him.

She held out her arms to her son. Irritation turned down the corners of her mouth. "To hear *you* talk, one would think so," she muttered just loud enough for him to hear.

"But you don't."

She paused to give him a look. "What I think," she enunciated clearly as she put her son in his car seat and strapped him in, "is that I have a tree to pick out for Miss Sadie, Mikey's fading fast and time is awastin'."

PRIOR TO MEETING Kevin McCabe, Noelle had thought she knew what it was to be pursued. She realized now she hadn't a clue.

"You must get lonely," he was saying. Mikey dozed on Kevin's shoulder as they strolled the aisles of the tree lot, perusing the various offerings.

Noelle checked the tag of one, the spread of branches on another, weighing the merits of each. "I admit living without a spouse—after you've been married—takes some getting used to. But I've done that and I like my independence."

Kevin glanced at her affectionately. "I wouldn't ever fence you in."

She tried not to smile. "Is that cowboy talk?"

"Courting," he corrected.

Wanting to keep the mood light, she batted her eyelashes at him flirtatiously. "Courting," she repeated dryly, wrapping her mind around that old-fashioned term. "So now we're courting?" And just how far was that from "seeing each other" or "dating?" Or, heaven help them, "hooking up?"

"Trying." He leaned close enough to whisper in her ear, "I don't seem to be getting very far."

Warming at the sensual promise in his tone, she said, "Maybe you should wish for something else for Christmas. Say that blonde over there by the cash register, the one in the Santa's helper hat. She's been eyeing you ever since we arrived."

Kevin was not the least bit interested. "I've known her since kindergarten," he said. "She's like a sister to me."

Pleased that Kevin seemed to have eyes only for her, Noelle pointed out playfully, "She's not looking at you like a sister."

Shifting closer, he buried his face in her hair. "Can we get back on track here?" he murmured softly.

Noelle tried—and failed—to put aside the memory of the passionate kisses they had shared so far. Just thinking about it made her hot and tingly all over. "I thought we were," she protested facetiously. "You want a woman for Christmas. And I'm trying to find you one."

Not to be dissuaded, Kevin stipulated, "Not just any woman."

"So you're picky." She regarded him with mock thoughtfulness.

"Very." Kevin kept his eyes on hers.

Noelle tapped her chin. "That could complicate matters somewhat," she warned, their breaths forming frosty puffs of air.

"I have every confidence I'll get what I want in the end," he told her assuredly.

Noelle savored the feeling of being there with him. "I hope you do," she said quietly, meaning it with all her heart. She stood on tiptoe and kissed him on his cheek. "Because bottom line, you're a good guy. And the good guys *always* deserve to win."

"YOU DON'T HAVE TO STAY and decorate the tree with me," Noelle said. "It was more than enough that you painted the steps while I made dinner, helped with Mikey's bath and bedtime routine and then carried the tree to the front porch."

Kevin took the lights out of the boxes he'd brought up from the basement, and began untangling them. "Hey, I'll do anything for cheese ravioli, green beans and applesauce."

Noelle unwrapped delicate glass ornaments that had been preserved in tissue paper, one by one. "Hard to tell who scarfed down more, you or Mikey."

Kevin aimed a thumb at the center of his chest. "We men have to keep up our strength when dealing with difficult women like you."

Her eyes widened in mock astonishment. "Difficult!" she bantered back affably. "Who are you calling difficult?"

He dropped what he was doing, closed the distance between them and wrapped his arms around her. "I think that would be you."

Enjoying their repartee as much as him, Noelle sank into the comforting warmth of his tall, strong body. He smelled and felt so good. "Why am I difficult?" she murmured against his chest.

Tightening his hold on her, he kissed his way down her neck. "Because you've only offered to be my friend."

He didn't know how much of a concession that

was on her part, given the fact he was a member of law enforcement who wanted a woman with a background every bit as squeaky clean and "implication free" as his own. Battling a self-conscious flush, she pulled away from him and went to make sure the tree was situated securely in the metal stand. Thanks to Kevin's earlier handiwork, it was. "Some men would think that was more than enough." She shrugged off his complaint as casually as she could.

Kevin brought a strand of lights over and began stringing them on the uppermost branches. He gave her a long look that spoke volumes. "Some men don't know a good thing when they see it."

Noelle pulled in a stabilizing breath. "Seriously, Kevin. I…"

"What?" he asked.

She wet her lips, tried again. "I don't think I have it in me to be the kind of girlfriend a man like you would need."

He leveled an assessing gaze on her and kept it there. "And what would that be, in your estimation?"

She swallowed around the sudden parched feeling in her throat. "Someone without any baggage."

"Back to the luggage again?" he replied in a way that made her heart skip first one beat, then another.

Noelle looked away. "I've had a lot of sadness in my life. It's been a struggle to get past it. It takes everything I have some days just to keep a smile on my face."

Kevin pressed his lips together ruefully and went to get another strand of lights. "See, that's where the problem is," he told her. "You won't let the joy in—even in this, of all seasons. You won't let a guy like me help you discover what it's like to let your guard down and be really and truly happy again."

Seeing he needed some help if they were ever going to finish in a timely manner, Noelle picked up the end of the strand he was wrapping and followed him around the tree. "Anyone ever told you that you're persistent?" she quipped, side-stepping his remark, which had cut too close to what was really going on with her.

Kevin glanced at her ruefully. "When I was five and fell off the roof and broke my arm." He sighed heavily. "But that's another story."

Curious to know what he had been like as a kid, Noelle asked, "What were you doing on the roof?"

A haunted look appeared in Kevin's eyes. "That's where *my* baggage comes in," he told her with a derisive shrug.

Noelle moved nearer, as they got to the end of the light string. "I think I'd like to hear about that."

He paused and looked down at her. "And spoil the jovial mood?"

They were standing so close she could feel the heat emanating from his powerful body. "Now who's evading?" she asked.

"It happened about a year after my mom died," he said finally. He walked over to get the last strand of lights to put on the tree. "I was missing her in the worst way. I knew she was in heaven, and I desperately wanted to see her and talk to her again. So I climbed out on the roof—thinking, with perfect five-year-old logic, that I might be able to see her better that way, or get to her, and next thing I know I'm in the E.R. and everyone is all upset."

Noelle could only imagine how terrible that must have been. She reached out and touched his arm. "That must have been so tough."

His expression turned brooding. "Probably the hardest thing I've ever been through," he admitted, his muscles tensing beneath her touch. A mixture of regret and self-admonition filled his tone as he continued, "Made all the more difficult by the idiocy of my dad, siblings and me."

Noelle felt a soul-deep ache at the pain in Kevin's voice. "I don't understand."

"We tried going it alone during the grieving process," Kevin said bitterly. "Thinking, in our strong, manly way, that it was best to just maintain that stiff upper lip and keep our feelings to ourselves. It took Kate Marten—the woman who is now my stepmom—coming in to help us, to make us understand that it's times when we feel most alone that we need to reach out to family and friends."

Noelle saw where this was going. The ramifications terrified her. "I have Dash and Miss Sadie and Mikey." Although only the prominent attorney knew her darkest secrets.

Kevin held her eyes for a long time. "And me."

Noelle edged away from the enticing woodsy scent of his cologne. "And you. For now."

Until you find out that my family background leaves a lot to be desired. Noelle didn't know much about the McCabes, but she did know the members of the prominent Texas family were famous for their honor and integrity. McCabes did not get serious about and marry people with haunting secrets and felony-laden pasts....

He caught her hand and reeled her in to his side. "For more than now," he said softly, "if you'll allow it."

Guilt over all she had yet to reveal brought a self-conscious flush to her cheeks.

"Come on a date with me, Noelle," he urged, wrapping an arm about her waist.

Noelle's heart pounded. She wanted to, so much! "I don't have a sitter."

Kevin shrugged. "You could always ask Dash."

Talk about turning the tables. "I don't think that's a good idea."

"You're probably right." He flashed her a sexy grin. "Best not to bring him into our relationship at all."

Aware he was going to be very hard to resist, Noelle asked, "What relationship?"

He brought her closer with slow deliberation. "The one we're starting."

Noelle's insides fluttered at the idea of making love with him. "Determination isn't always a virtue."

He kissed her temple and the curve of her cheek. "Sure it is."

"I don't even know where you live," she protested breathlessly.

He let her go, as abruptly as he had taken her into his arms, and went back to stringing lights on the tree. "That can be remedied easily enough. Bring Mikey into town tomorrow. I get off at five. We can have dinner at my house. I'll cook—something with cheese and green beans and applesauce. And then we'll take Mikey to the live nativity scene in front of Laramie Community Church."

She laughed at the G-rated nature of the proposed date. It wasn't exactly what she had been expecting.

He gazed at her confidently. "You're going to say yes, aren't you?"

How could she not? "Against my better judgment, probably." Noelle placed several crystal ornaments on the branches, then glanced at him warily. "But I'm only agreeing to dinner and seeing the nativity lights, so it's not going to be a very long date."

"At this point, I'll take what I can get," he drawled. "Meanwhile, you've got a problem. How are you going to keep Mikey away from the Christmas tree?"

Noelle bit her lip. "I'll have to keep him out of this room entirely, from now on. If he were to grab a crystal ornament…"

"It could easily break."

"And we don't want that," Noelle finished.

"Any more than we want to deprive Mikey of

the experience of having a child-safe tree he can enjoy." A thoughtful silence fell between them. Kevin laced his arm around her waist. "You could let him help decorate the tree at my place with toddler-friendly decorations."

Once again he had surprised—and delighted—her with the depth of his concern for her and her son. "And you wouldn't mind?"

"It'd be fun." The cell phone clipped to his belt began to ring. Frowning, Kevin answered it. "McCabe." He listened, then spoke in a brisk businesslike tone. "That's great. I'll be there as soon as I can...probably around midnight." He ended the connection.

"What's up?" Noelle asked.

"The Houston Police Department just arrested the mastermind of the identity theft ring," Kevin told her grimly. "I'm going to drive down and talk to him tonight."

KEVIN STARED AT THE mop-haired kid on the other side of the one-way glass. This could not really be The Wizard. Could it? "How old is he?"

The HPD detective replied, "Sixteen."

"You thinking what I'm thinking?" Kevin asked his colleague.

"Mmm-hmm. Unfortunately, he's not been inclined to talk to any of us. Given the results you used to have when it came to getting troubled kids to open up…"

"I'll give it my best effort," Kevin promised. "Has he asked for an attorney yet?"

"No. His parents know he's here—Mr. and Mrs. Roth have a team with search warrants at their house right now. They've sent an attorney. He should be here soon."

Which meant there wasn't much time to make inroads with the kid, since the first thing an attorney would do was tell Scooter not to say one more word to the police.

Kevin walked in. "Hi, Scooter. I'm Detective McCabe from the Laramie Sheriff's Department."

Scooter's expression went from scared to belligerent. "Why are you here?" he demanded. "I've never even been to Laramie."

"One of the victims is Sadie Nelson. She has

homes in Houston and Laramie. I think you know her."

"Yeah." Scooter ducked his head.

Kevin pulled up a chair. "She's a real nice lady. Does a lot of good work for a lot of different charities. Hard to imagine anyone wanting to upset her so much she'd fall and break her leg and end up in a nursing home."

Scooter's eyes widened with concern. "Is she going to be okay?"

Kevin lifted a hand. "Her body will heal. I don't know about her heart."

Scooter stared at the table, swallowed hard.

Kevin leaned forward. He dropped his voice to a confidential whisper. "Here's the thing, Scooter. A lot of money was stolen. Right now, everyone is fingering you. As the brilliant mind behind the theft, you're liable to get the maximum punishment. On the other hand, if you're just the scapegoat—the messenger, as it were—and if you cooperate with us and help us find the real culprit, then I promise you I'll do everything I can to make sure the judge is lenient with you."

Scooter's hands shook. "Am I going to have to go to jail?"

Not about to sugarcoat it for the kid, Kevin nodded grimly. "The only question is for how long."

The door to the interrogation room opened. A tall man in a suit walked in. "Scooter, not another word," he said firmly, then turned to Kevin. "I'm the boy's lawyer. His parents have retained me to represent him."

"I CAN'T BELIEVE Scooter Roth would steal from anyone, never mind me!" Miss Sadie declared late the next morning, when Kevin stopped by Laramie Gardens to bring her up to speed on the latest developments in her identity theft case. "I bought Christmas decorations from Scooter earlier in the fall!"

"Did you want those on the Christmas tree?" Noelle asked. "Because I didn't see anything new...."

"That's because I haven't received them yet," Miss Sadie replied. "There was a problem with the delivery. I wasn't going to be in town when the decorations came in, so I asked Scooter to hold them for me until I contacted him. He said I could just e-mail him when I wanted him to come by with them, but I don't have e-mail. So I was just going to call when I returned from my cruise."

Which explained, Kevin thought, how Scooter and his partners in crime knew Miss Sadie was vulnerable to identity theft. Scooter, it seemed, had definitely fed someone that information. "Did you ever notice Scooter hanging around a bad crowd?" Kevin asked. "Or spending a lot of money? Did he have a penchant for partying?"

"No," Miss Sadie replied thoughtfully. "If anything, Scooter was almost too quiet. Sometimes I'd see him out riding his skateboard around the neighborhood and he looked like he had the weight of the world on his shoulders. But there's no doubt he was bright. His parents expected him to go to Harvard when the time came." Miss Sadie laid a frail hand across her heart. "Merilee and Phil must be beside themselves."

Kevin frowned. "I don't know what the Roths'

reaction was—I didn't have a chance to meet them. But they hired a fine criminal lawyer for him."

"Poor kid," Noelle murmured, the distant look back in her eyes. "You said he's only what—sixteen? To be in such a mess, his whole future wrecked…"

"Scooter Roth might be young and scared right now, but he's no innocent," Kevin countered sternly. "He was caught sending those e-mails with further instructions regarding the stolen goods, and the computer in his room at home was jam-packed with other proof demonstrating that he was responsible for setting up the accounts. He and his band of thieves have wrecked a lot of lives, at least in the short term, until we get everyone's credit straightened out."

"Do you really think he thought up this elaborate scam all by himself?" Noelle asked skeptically.

"What makes you think he didn't?" Kevin countered, watching the play of emotions on her pretty face.

"I don't know. It's just a hunch," she replied. "I

think Scooter might have had some help some-where along the way, getting in this mess."

"As it happens, we do think he's protecting someone," Kevin allowed.

"Any idea who?" she asked.

"Nope. And unfortunately, thanks to that fancy lawyer his parents hired, Scooter's already out of juvie and home with his parents, to await trial."

Noelle blinked in surprise. "You're kidding! Scooter's already been arraigned?"

Once again, he couldn't help noticing that Noelle displayed a startling amount of knowl-edge compared to the average layperson not con-nected with law enforcement. On the other hand, he reasoned, she was close friends with a lawyer—albeit Dash Nelson was a civil litigator not a criminal attorney.

"Apparently, his parents are quite prominent, and strings were pulled to expedite the process," Kevin replied.

"Why don't you think it's a good thing for Scooter to be home with Merilee and Phil as soon as possible?" Miss Sadie interrupted.

Kevin frowned. "Putting Scooter back in his normal environment will allow him to downplay the seriousness of his situation, at least in his own view. If he had stayed in juvie even a few more days, I think the reality would hit him a lot harder. He'd have a better chance of making an informed decision about whether or not he wants to cooperate with law enforcement in identifying the person or persons who set all this up."

"Have you spoken to his folks about this?" Miss Sadie asked, her concern for the boy equal to Noelle's.

Kevin shook his head. "Right now, the Roths are not talking to anyone in the department, on the advice of their lawyer. I'm hoping that will change as the holiday nears and they come to grips with the strength of the case against their son."

After all the excitement, Miss Sadie declared herself parched and a little hungry, and she was sure they were, too. Noelle and Kevin walked with Mikey down to the snack area to get everyone apple juice and cookies.

"Do you know the Roths?" Kevin asked, taking several individual cartons out of the fridge.

She loaded up on packets of vanilla shortbread. "No. I've never done any parties for them. I don't know Scooter, either. I'm glad you're on his side, though. He needs someone determined to get to the truth, whether he cooperates or not."

Kevin picked up some paper napkins. Curious but not surprised about the depth of her compassion, he remarked, "Truth is important to you, hmm?"

"I can't stand to see anyone become a scapegoat for someone else," she said bluntly, her expression troubled. "It's doubly unfair when it's a kid being taken advantage of."

Kevin felt the same way. That was one of the reasons he'd become a detective. So he could make sure investigations were done properly and that innocent people weren't put on trial. "Sure you didn't miss your calling?" he asked warmly. "Maybe you should have been a child advocate or guardian ad litem instead of an event planner."

Noelle let his suggestion pass without comment. "Speaking of events," she said matter-of-factly, handing the snacks to Kevin and taking a suddenly rambunctious Mikey's hand in hers. "Can I count on you to help decorate the community center later this week?"

"From five on," Kevin promised, as the three of them headed back toward Miss Sadie's room. "Until then I'm on duty. What about you?" He paused just outside the door, longing for more time alone with Noelle. "We still on for our date this evening?"

Noelle regarded him thoughtfully. "You're not too tired to cook?"

Kevin smiled. "Come on over and see."

Chapter Eight

Kevin McCabe's house turned out to be a pleasant surprise. The bungalow had recently undergone extensive renovation, and everything in it, from the wood floors to built-in cabinetry, gleamed with a soft golden patina. The furnishings were sparse but masculine. And yet it was a very toddler-friendly place. No breakables within reach; no sharp edges to worry about. The leather sofa and chairs were heavily cushioned, would withstand a lot of climbing up and down, and could easily be wiped clean.

And the inviting ambiance didn't stop there, Noelle noted happily. Kevin had placed a small tree in a bucket of sand that made it virtually tip proof. The fragrance of fresh-cut pine filled the air. Christmas music played softly on the stereo.

"I hope you two brought your appetites," Kevin said with a twinkle, leading them into the spacious kitchen. He had borrowed a booster chair for Mikey.

Noelle looked at the chili simmering in a Crock-Pot on the counter, the green beans on the stove and the golden cornbread baking in the oven. Bite-size cheese quesadillas, in the shape of animals, had just come off the griddle.

Her admiration grew when she noticed the plate of delicate pastries covered with confectioner's sugar. "Are those apple fritters?"

Kevin held up a hand to stave off compliments. "I've got to confess," he said with a self-effacing grin, "I didn't make those. I got them from my aunt Greta, over at the Lone Star Dance Hall. She told me they were a kid favorite and could be warmed in the oven or microwave. But the rest is my cooking."

"Do you realize you are the first man who has ever cooked for me?"

He looked as pleased as she felt. "Does that give me extra brownie points?" Taking the quesadillas off the stove to cool, he went to the fridge and brought out a jug of milk.

"Yes. *A* for effort. As for the taste…" Noelle teased, settling her son at the round oak kitchen table, "I am sure Mikey will let us know."

As it turned out, he was ecstatic. Mikey demolished everything on his plate, while Noelle and Kevin did similar damage to theirs. "This was absolutely wonderful," she praised when the delicious meal had concluded. She was very glad she had decided to accept his invitation and have dinner there that evening. "Thank you for going to so much trouble and making all of Mikey's favorite foods."

Kevin handed her a damp washcloth. "You're welcome."

Noelle washed Mikey's face and hands. She lifted him out of the chair and set him down on the floor. "You're going to have to give me the recipe for the chili." She watched as the boy toddled off to explore the kitchen cabinets, all of which had been tied shut.

"I'd like to," Kevin replied, watching as Mikey tried and failed to figure out how to get them open. Returning his attention to Noelle, he wrapped his arms around her waist and drew her against him. "But it's a secret." He leaned down to whisper in her ear. "To enjoy it again, you'll just have to come over here."

The chili had been hot and delicious. It was nothing compared to the feel of him pressed up against her. "That sounds like blackmail."

He considered that with a mischievous glint in his eyes. "More like an invitation."

As their gazes met, Noelle felt a shiver slip through her. Trying not to notice how cozy it felt to be in close proximity with Kevin, she said, "You'd really want us hanging around?"

Smug male confidence radiated from him. "What do you think?"

He bent his head and delivered a steamy kiss. Noelle murmured her assent. Kevin deepened the kiss and pulled her closer, the pressure of his hands on her spine bringing her intimately near. A torrent of need swept through her, sending all her senses into an uproar. Her pleasure was interrupted only by the feel of a small car being driven over her knee. She and Kevin broke contact and looked down, but did not move apart, since Mikey gripped both their legs.

"Hi." Their tiny chaperone grinned.

"Hi," both said in unison.

"I think that means it's time to decorate the Christmas tree," Kevin murmured.

She looked at the cluttered countertops and uncleared table. "The dishes—"

"Can wait. Let's just enjoy our time with Mikey."

Definitely, Noelle thought, a man after her own heart.

Together, the three of them went into the living room and opened the box of toddler-friendly ornaments. Kevin showed Mikey how to fit the large plastic hooks over the branches. Noelle was pleased to see that her son got the hang of decorating right away. She sat on the floor, handing Mikey one unbreakable ornament after another. "This was a really good idea. I can't believe how much he is enjoying it."

"Now all we need is a digital camera so you can capture the moment on film."

Noelle had been so excited about the date she had forgotten to bring hers. "Do you have one?"

"Right here." Kevin handed it to her and watched as she snapped picture after picture. Motioning for her to move next to her son, he got down on one knee and snapped several photos of them together. "I'll get some prints made up for you," he promised.

"Thank you. In the meantime—" Noelle turned her affectionate gaze from Kevin to her son "—at least we know what Mikey's new favorite thing is." She smiled as he took a kid-on-a-sled ornament off the tree and replaced it with a snowman in a top hat.

KEVIN KNEW WHAT HIS NEW favorite thing was, too. Spending time with Noelle and her son. Being with them this way gave him a new understanding of the meaning of family. It explained why his brothers who were married and had kids looked so happy all the time. Riley and Brad had tried to explain how content they were, being husbands and fathers. Now, finally, Kevin understood what they meant.

Noelle tucked her hand in his and turned to him with a smile. "What was your favorite thing about the holiday?" she asked.

That, Kevin thought, was easy. "The family being together. Still is."

Her smile faded slightly.

Guilt overwhelmed him. Talk about spoiling the mood, he noted, as she withdrew her hand from his. "I'm sorry," he said softly. "I didn't mean to say anything to upset you."

"It's okay. I've dealt with the loss of my husband. I'm ready to move on."

Kevin was glad to hear that. "What's your favorite thing about Christmas?" he asked, determined to get the joy back in the conversation.

"Right now, the look in Mikey's eyes." Noelle cast another affectionate glance at her son. "I can't wait for Christmas morning. He's going to be so excited."

"I'll bet," Kevin murmured. He smiled as

Mikey handed him an ornament he had just taken from the tree, then toddled back to get another.

"So what was your favorite Christmas, growing up?" Noelle asked, watching while Mikey removed another one, then brought it to her.

"I don't know if I can choose the best one," Kevin said. "All the ones we had when my mom was alive were great, and so were the ones after Kate married my dad and joined our family. But the year without either my mom or my stepmom really bit. We were all so sad. We didn't celebrate the holiday at all. We just wanted it to be over. What about you?"

"That's easy." Noelle rested her hand on his thigh. "The year my parents and I lived in Sun Valley, Idaho."

Alarm bells went off in Kevin's head. There had been nothing in the background check he had done that indicated Noelle and her parents had lived anywhere but Houston. That didn't mean they hadn't. Her father had been an engineer and could have accepted a temporary work assignment without ever giving up his home or changing his residency. Kevin knew the records he had looked at would not necessarily have reflected that. "How old were you?" he asked, covering her hand with his own.

"Five or six. It was my last year to believe in the existence of jolly old—" Noelle stopped speaking abruptly and cast a glance at Mikey "—well, you know who. And it was my first year to see snow on Christmas Eve, which added such a magical dimension." She paused, gratitude shining in her eyes. "I'm so glad you offered to help arrange for Mikey to see snow. I'm still not sure how you're going to manage it."

"It wouldn't be a surprise if I told you," Kevin reminded her.

She tapped her index finger against her lips. "I heard it snowed here last year, on Christmas Eve."

Kevin nodded. "For the first time in ten years."

"And that your brother Riley and his wife, Amanda, actually went to the church to say their vows in a horse-drawn sleigh," she continued, impressed.

"Also true." It had been a very romantic—and

memorable—occasion. "Sad to say, I doubt we can count on Old Man Weather cooperating with us again this year…since that happens so rarely."

"Hmm." She narrowed her eyes at him. "Now you're really making me curious."

"What can I tell you?" Kevin grinned. "It helps to be connected in this town. But I promise you that on December twenty-third, the night of the community center party, it will be snowing in Laramie."

"This year is shaping up to be my best holiday ever," Noelle declared, getting up to hand Mikey an ornament he couldn't quite reach.

"Even better than the one in Sun Valley?" Kevin asked curiously.

"Absolutely." Noelle beamed. "And I've got to tell you, I had kind of given up hope that would ever happen."

Realizing this was his chance to clear up any inconsistencies in what he knew about her, Kevin said casually, "I didn't realize you had lived in the north."

Noelle sat down next to the Christmas tree. "Where did you think I lived?" she asked.

Guilt rushed through him once again, trumped by the even stronger need to know the truth. "I don't know," he fibbed with a shrug. "Houston?"

She shook her head. "That's where I've lived the last eight years. When I was growing up, my family moved frequently, usually about once a year."

"Did your dad work for the military or something?" Kevin knew that could explain it. Civilian subcontractors sometimes had to move around as much as their commissioned counterparts.

Oblivious to the fact he had done a background check on her within hours after they had first met, Noelle shook her head again. "Real estate. My dad was an appraiser, my mother a sales agent."

Okay, that was definitely not meshing with the public records Kevin had seen. It didn't mean he had to panic, or brand her a liar, he told himself sternly. "I thought real estate professionals had to stay put, to build up a clientele."

"That's true for most. But then you have to deal with the downturns in the market. My parents didn't want to do that so they moved wherever the boom was, and when it looked like it had peaked, they picked up and moved to the next hot spot."

Made sense. "So they were licensed in a lot of different states."

"Yes."

Knowing he would figure out the reason behind the discrepancy sooner or later, Kevin kept pressing for details. The truth was there somewhere; he just had to find it. "Ever thought of going into real estate yourself?" he asked.

"No. They wanted me to but it just wasn't for me." Without warning, the faraway look was back in her eyes. Kevin had the sense she was withholding something, deliberately keeping him at bay once again.

"Why did you become a cop?" Noelle switched the subject adroitly, helping Mikey retrieve and then rehang another ornament on the tree.

Reminded of another time and a similar situation that had not raised his suspicions—not at first, anyway—Kevin ignored the knot in his gut and answered her question pleasantly. "I was always interested in law enforcement, from the time I was little. Whenever we played pretend, I was the policeman or sheriff. As I got older, I found myself more and more in the role of enforcer slash peacemaker."

Noelle busied herself helping her son decorate and redecorate the tree. "Favorite part of the job?"

That, at least, was easy. "Making sure the law is followed. Knowing the order that it brings."

"Least favorite part?" she said even more softly.

Aware he wanted her to confide in him more than ever, Kevin said, "Having people look me in the eye sometimes and lie to me outright, then expect I'll do nothing about it."

KEVIN'S DELIBERATELY uttered words were like a kick to Noelle's gut. This was a nightmare—wanting so badly to be close to him, yet unable to tell him everything about herself, for reasons that had seemed valid at the time but now grew more questionable every day. The worst part of it was, she didn't want to go back to where she had been or claim her past. And yet she was beginning to see that she would never be able to completely escape it.

"For instance," Kevin continued amiably, coming over to sit next to her and Mikey, "periodically the county sets up roadblocks at night and checks for drunk driving. That's not my favorite thing to do, but I know it saves lives. So we do it. And it never fails—we'll pull over someone who's obviously inebriated and they'll swear up and down they haven't had anything to drink. Then it'll turn out their blood alcohol level is three times the legal limit, and they'll show up in court and swear the lab was wrong. Fortunately, these days we have videotape sobriety tests, and once the judge or jury sees that, it's usually a clear-cut case for a conviction."

Noelle admired his dedication to upholding the law, even as she feared the more curious side of him. She brought her knees up to her chest and wrapped her arms around them. "It must make you feel good, when you get somebody off the road who clearly shouldn't be driving."

Kevin nodded and regarded her with barely checked affection. "So what's the best thing about your job?"

Noelle pretended an insouciance she couldn't begin to feel. "I love it when an event comes together and everyone has a great time. Memories are made."

"Worst part?" He moved closer and took her hand in his.

She could feel the blood rushing to her cheeks even as she struggled to get a grip on her soaring emotions. "When everything that can go wrong does and we spend the evening narrowly averting one catastrophe after another."

"And yet still manage to pull off a wonderful event," he guessed.

"Usually that is the case," Noelle admitted.

"When given lemons, make lemonade."

She nodded, aware the two of them were very much in agreement about that. "It's a lesson I learned early in my adult life." Her cell phone rang just then. She went to get it out of her purse and looked at the caller ID. "Do you mind?" she asked Kevin with a frown. "It's business."

"Go ahead."

Noelle listened to the Houston hotel manager,

then groaned. "Tell me this is an early April fool's joke," she pleaded.

"It's not an early April fool's joke. Due to an outage of our computer system last October, we accidentally double booked the hotel ballroom for the night of January fifteenth. And since the other event is a fund-raiser for the president of the United States..."

"You expect Miss Sadie's charity to bow out."

"We can help you find an alternate site for the black-tie event that same night."

Already switching to business mode, Noelle listened to the three possibilities mentioned. "I'm not familiar with two of the ballrooms you've mentioned," she said.

"They'll give you a better price deal than the first."

Atmosphere, not cost, was Miss Sadie's bottom line. "I'm going to have to take a look," Noelle said.

"Again," the manager soothed, "we are so sorry."

"So am I." She hung up the phone with a beleaguered sigh, then briefly she explained the situation to Kevin. "I can't believe it. I'm going to have to drive back to Houston tonight." She ran her hands through her hair.

Kevin studied her, seeming to know intuitively how much she disliked driving long distances late at night, especially over largely rural roads. "Want me to follow you in my car or go with you?" He stood. "I wanted to have a talk with Scooter Roth and his parents, anyway."

Noelle gathered up her coat and Mikey's. "You wouldn't mind?"

"Not a bit," Kevin assured her. "But first, let's take Mikey to see that nativity scene, as promised."

IT WAS AFTER MIDNIGHT by the time Kevin and Noelle parked their vehicles in front of her Houston town home and got out. Mikey was sleeping soundly in his car seat. He looked like an angel in his fleece sleeper, his blanket and favorite stuffed animal tucked in around him. Knowing the little boy was an armful, even when not sound asleep, Kevin asked. "Do you want me to carry him in for you?"

She shot Kevin a grateful glance. "I want to try not to wake him, if at all possible," she cautioned.

"I'll do my best," he promised.

Looking beautiful but weary, Noelle leaned into the car to unfasten the straps on Mikey's seat. After she handed him over to Kevin's waiting arms, the two adults moved soundlessly up the sidewalk to the front door. Kevin waited while Noelle slid her key in the lock and swung the glossy cranberry-red door open. His shoulder brushed the evergreen wreath as he stepped inside. He noticed that Noelle had a tree up. Like the one Kevin had selected for his house, it was child-size and decorated with ribbons and child-safe ornaments. Unlike his, hers was artificial.

Noelle led the way up the stairs to a bedroom just past the master suite. The nursery was decorated with a truck motif, as were the linens on Mikey's crib. Kevin handed the boy back to Noelle and she tucked him in his bed. After turning on the night-light and baby monitor, she stood there a moment looking down at him.

The love she felt for her son was a palpable presence in the room.

The surprising thing was that Kevin felt it, too.

FIGURING HE WOULD HELP her out as much as he could before they said good-night, Kevin carried Noelle's laptop computer, briefcase and diaper bag inside for her. He found her standing in front of the refrigerator, hands propped on her hips, a distressed look on her face.

"What's wrong?" he asked.

She sighed and ran a hand through her curls. "I forgot I don't have any milk or juice here."

That was easy enough to fix. "I can go get some for you."

She turned. "You've done so much already, Kevin."

"Really, I don't mind."

A smile spread across her face, even as she glided toward him. "I don't know why I keep letting you become so indispensable to me," she murmured in a low, wistful voice he found even sexier than the way she looked.

"Sure you do." Giving in to impulse, he took her in his arms, kissed her gently, persuasively, until she kissed him back as thoroughly as he was kissing her. "You have a damsel-in-distress complex," he teased.

Noelle tensed, as if he'd struck a nerve. Wanting her to know he was just kidding, he continued affably, "All women secretly want to be rescued by a big, strong man who also happens to have the hots for them."

"I gather we're talking about someone specific here?"

He tugged her closer still. "Um-hmm. Me." He kissed his way down her neck, deciding she felt so deliciously warm and right he didn't want to ever let her go. "And you."

Noelle moaned. "Kevin…"

"I know." He dragged his thumb across her lip. "I really have to be leaving." He hugged her close, breathing in the fragrance of her hair.

"That wasn't what I was saying." A breathless silence strung out between them, until he drew back, looked down into her face. "I was going to say I wanted you to stay."

Chapter Nine

Kevin stared at Noelle, hardly believing his ears. He had been hoping for just this sort of reaction from her.

"There's no reason for you to check into a hotel. You should sleep here tonight," she continued softly. "I'll pull out the sofa bed for you."

So much for the wish for an impetuous holiday fling, he thought ruefully.

Not about to pass up the chance to spend time with her and get to know her better, he checked his desire, figuring there would be plenty of time for that later. "Thanks. I'd like that. Meantime, I better go pick up the milk and juice Mikey is going to need come morning."

All-business once again, Noelle reached for a

notepad and pen. "Let me give you directions to the closest twenty-four hour grocery store."

Twenty minutes later, Kevin was back, groceries in hand.

He walked in to find the sofa bed in the living room already made up, a candy cane and a note from Noelle on his pillow. "Better get some shut-eye," she had written. "Mikey wakes early…."

Kevin went to sleep fantasizing about what it would be like to be an integral part of Noelle and Mikey's life. He woke at 6:00 a.m. as a pair of footsteps padded downstairs, one step at a time. Opening his eyes, he caught a glimpse of a yawning Noelle holding on to her son's hand. She was wearing a pink spaghetti-strapped tank top and matching pajama cardigan that made the most of her full breasts and slender torso. Pink-and-white flannel pajama bottoms warmed her long slender legs, fluffy pink slippers her feet. With her hair tousled and her cheeks rosy from sleep, she was undoubtedly the sexiest woman he had ever seen. As well as the most patient, loving mother…

The minute they hit the ground floor, Mikey

raced toward him, a toy truck in his hand. "Monster tick-up-puck!" he announced, waving his toy and peering into Kevin's face. "Right?"

Grinning, he nodded. "Right. That's a monster pickup truck."

"Pick-up-puck!" Mikey repeated enthusiastically, vaulting up on the sofa bed. He scrambled onto Kevin's chest. "Monster pick-up-puck!"

"Mikey, honey…" Noelle approached, apology in her voice, a mixture of amusement and affection in her eyes. "It's awfully early. Kevin hasn't even had any coffee."

Seeing Noelle was all the wake-up call he needed. "It's okay." Kevin chuckled while Mikey patted his face. "Like I said, I've got a lot of nieces and nephews."

His expression intent, Mikey ran his monster truck across Kevin's chest, down his arm, back up to his shoulder.

Exasperated but content to let the situation play out as it would, Noelle disappeared into the kitchen. When she returned a few minutes later with a steaming mug of coffee for Kevin, she looked considerably more awake. "Mikey, your breakfast is ready." She held out her hand to her son. "You can bring your truck."

He toddled off with her.

Grateful for the momentary privacy, Kevin got up and pulled on his jeans and the sweater he'd been wearing the night before. "Feel free to use the guest bath upstairs," Noelle called from the other room. "Breakfast won't be ready for another fifteen minutes."

Breakfast. Made for him by the woman of his dreams. Contentment flowed through him. He could get used to this.

"DASH." Noelle stared at her old friend in the doorway. His timing couldn't be worse.

"I know it's early." Dash held up a silencing hand. "But I got your message and I wanted to talk to you before I headed to court."

Noelle caught the curious glance of one of her neighbors, heading to his car. Wishing she had on something other than her pajamas, she stepped aside. "Come on in."

As she shut the door behind him, Dash glanced at the rumpled covers on the sofa bed. "Everything okay?" he asked, concerned.

"Yes." She might as well tell him. He'd find out soon enough, anyway. "Kevin McCabe bunked here last night."

Dash paused, offered a tactful smile. "If I'd known he needed a place to stay, I would have put him up."

Noelle nodded as graciously as possible. "I'll tell him. I'm sure he'll be happy to know that." Mindful of the reason Dash was there, Noelle went to her desk and got out the file on the January fifteenth charity event. "There's a penalty clause in the contract with the hotel that reneged on us," she explained, as she handed it over. "They owe us twenty-five percent of the cost should they fail to provide the agreed upon services. I figured you'd want to handle this for Miss Sadie."

"Thanks. I do." Dash gave it a cursory glance, then closed the file. In no hurry to depart, he braced a shoulder against the wall. "How did my aunt take the bad news?"

Noelle grimaced. "I haven't told her yet. I wanted to get another ballroom lined up for her approval before broaching the subject."

"Otherwise she would just worry," Dash said.

"And it's been a rough enough month for her already," Noelle concurred. "In any case, I should have everything arranged by late today. As always, I'll fax any and all contracts to your office for your perusal before I ask Miss Sadie to sign them."

"Thanks." Dash knelt as Mikey toddled toward him. He returned the little boy's hug affectionately and then stood. "How long are you going to be in town?"

"Hopefully, just until tomorrow morning." Noelle watched Mikey take his toy truck over to the sofa bed. "I really need to get back to Laramie. I still have a lot to do there, and I like being able to take Mikey over to see Miss Sadie and check in on her every day. Especially given the fact she was betrayed by her neighbor. She's very upset about that. She still can't believe Scooter Roth did it, never mind was the mastermind of such an insidious plan."

"From what Aunt Sadie told me, I'd have to agree." Dash paused, compassion etched on his face. "I figured you'd be upset." His voice lowered confidentially. "Just because…"

"It was so close to what happened to me," Noelle whispered back.

"Yes." A painful silence fell between them.

She looked up at Dash. "I don't know what I would have done if you hadn't stepped in and helped me back then," she told him gratefully.

His expression turned protective. "I wasn't about to let you take the fall for something you didn't do. Any more than I want anything to hurt you now."

"Initially, I was under suspicion in this case, you know."

Dash froze. "Are you still?"

"I don't know." Noelle hesitated. Being around law enforcement still left her feeling edgy and on guard. "I think I've been able to set Kevin's mind at ease. But sometimes…the way he looks at me…" She shrugged, not sure she could put her feelings into words.

Dash's brow lifted. "You think McCabe suspects?"

"Suspects what?" Kevin asked smoothly, strolling in.

"WHAT SHE'S PLANNING to give you for Christmas," Dash replied after a short but telling pause.

Kevin wasn't sure what Noelle and Dash had been discussing—he'd only caught the tail end of their conversation. He knew it wasn't something either of them wanted him to witness. Dash's expression was lawyer-bland, giving away absolutely nothing. In contrast, the look on Noelle's face was guilty as all get-out. The two were definitely hiding something that he was certain had nothing to do with gift selection.

Unease sifted through him. Had he let his emotions get in the way, and ruled out both Noelle and Dash in the identity-theft case way too soon?

Kevin looked at Noelle, who was suddenly back in the kitchen, making more coffee. "I didn't realize we were exchanging gifts," he stated, watching her reaction carefully.

She forced a smile and cut him a glance that didn't quite meet his eyes. "I thought Mikey and I should do something for you—the spirit of Christmas, the season of giving and all that."

Kevin didn't want to pass on the opportunity to spend time with Noelle and her son, although he could see Dash was less than pleased with the notion. "Sounds fun," he said.

Flustered, Noelle looked at the unopened carton of eggs next to the stove. "Breakfast will be ready in a minute…"

Kevin wished he could stay. "Sorry. I'm going to have to pass," he told her reluctantly. "The Roths have agreed to see me but only if I can get to their place before Scooter has to leave for school."

Dash took off his jacket and sat at the table. "I've got time," he said, making himself comfortable.

Kevin frowned. It figured. But the quest for Noelle's time and attention wasn't over yet.

ON THE SURFACE, Kevin noted, the Roths looked like any other well-to-do family. "Mom" and "Dad" looked polished and professional in designer suits and expensive shoes. Their home was large and beautifully furnished, right down to the priceless antiques and the expensive art on the wall, and their manner was gracious. Yet something about them didn't ring true to Kevin from the very first. It was almost as if the Roths thought they were more clever than the police and were going to be able to schmooze their way out of this mess their son was in. Their attorney, a noted criminal defense lawyer, was every bit as slick. Only Scooter—in his private-school uniform, hair hanging down in his face—seemed uncertain about his fate.

"You should know, Detective, we're talking to the district attorney about a plea deal," the lawyer began.

Mr. and Mrs. Roth both nodded emphatically. "Scooter has learned his lesson," Mrs. Roth swore. "No more betting over the Internet with cyber bookies. And certainly no more criminal activity to pay off his debts."

"We're all going to cooperate to the fullest extent of the law," her husband agreed, putting one arm around her waist, while Scooter slumped even lower in his wing chair.

"Unfortunately, they've already told all they know," the attorney remarked. "Scooter merely e-mailed the instructions and information given him, in order to keep the vicious thugs from hunting him down. It looks as if the mysterious ringleader—The Wizard, as he or she liked to be called—may never be caught."

Kevin continued making notes on the pad in front of him. "I wouldn't bet on that. The case is far from closed. And won't be until we identify The Wizard."

Interestingly enough, Scooter's parents look scared by Kevin's declaration, while the boy seemed almost relieved to know law enforcement was still involved. Which meant the threat was very real.

Kevin looked at Scooter. "I know you don't want to rat anyone else out, but sometimes you have to think about protecting yourself. This is one of those times. Whether or not The Wizard is found, you're facing some serious jail time."

"I think we might be able to get a deal with the district attorney for probation," Scooter's attorney said.

"You should know, Scooter," Kevin warned frankly, "the district attorney can make a recommendation to the court regarding sentencing. That doesn't mean the judge has to abide by it. No deal is a sure thing."

"Stop trying to frighten him unnecessarily," Mrs. Roth declared.

Kevin took his business card out of his pocket. He stood and handed it to Scooter. "Sometimes you know more than you think. If you remember anything else, or recall anything that might help, you can phone me anytime." He looked Scooter right in the eye. "At the end of the day, the best person to help you out of this mess you're in is not a parent or your lawyer. It's you."

AT NINE O'CLOCK that night, Noelle was just starting her workout when her doorbell rang.

Kevin McCabe was standing on the porch. "I

wanted to stop by and see if there was anything else you needed before I headed back to Laramie."

Aware of the brisk air sweeping in, Noelle ushered him inside and shut the door. Her yoga mat lay in the middle of the living room floor and the television showed an instructor demonstrating "the tree."

Kevin paused and looked at the screen. "Can you actually do that stuff?"

Noelle grinned and adopted the position, one foot pressed against the upper thigh of her other leg, hands pressed together prayerlike in front of her. "Yes. It's fun…and relaxing."

He regarded her drolly. "I'll take your word for it."

Aware she was tingling all over, and not from the workout she had just begun, Noelle picked up the remote and hit the stop button.

"So is there anything you need before I leave the city?" Kevin repeated.

Noelle smiled, a little embarrassed at just how happy she was to see him. "We're fine. Mikey and I are driving back to Laramie first thing in the morning. But if you've got a few minutes—" she led the way into her kitchen "—I wouldn't mind hearing how your meeting with Scooter Roth and his parents went."

Finding she was suddenly parched, Noelle took a pitcher of lemon water out of the fridge and poured two glasses. After she handed him one, Kevin settled against the counter.

"We still think all three of them know much more than they are letting on," he said, "and could if not identify the ringleader, at least give us some idea where to look."

"But they're not cooperating," Noelle guessed.

Kevin appeared just as concerned as she felt. "Mr. and Mrs. Roth are banking on a deal with the district attorney. I don't think that's going to keep Scooter out of jail, and I told them so."

"But it didn't make any difference."

"Not to Mr. and Mrs. Roth," he replied.

"What about Scooter? Did he take you seriously?"

Kevin let out a disgruntled sigh. "Maybe. In any case, he knows how to reach me if he 'thinks of anything'." He took a long drink, wiped the corner of his mouth with the back of his hand. "In the meantime, we're still investigating. I spent the day interviewing the others awaiting trial and got some more information."

"Thanks for the update."

"No problem. So, Dash isn't here?" Kevin asked casually, looking past Noelle.

"Funny," she replied dryly. "Dash asked the same thing about you not too long ago. He stopped by after work to see how things were going with me and Mikey."

Kevin shrugged. "Great minds think alike."

She continued to study him. "Don't you mean competing minds think alike?"

Kevin nonchalantly drained the rest of his drink and set the glass down. "Not sure I know what you mean."

"I think you do, Detective." Noelle angled her chin. "I think Mikey and I have somehow become a 'territory' thing between you and Dash, and the two of you are doing the equivalent of peeing in the corners."

Kevin threw back his head and laughed. "Great analogy."

She stomped closer, until they were standing close enough to feel each other's body heat. "Can you tell me you weren't hoping to interrupt—or thwart—something between Dash and me tonight…if he had happened to be here?"

The mischief in Kevin's eyes faded, replaced by something much more acute. "I'm not going to pretend I don't want you all to myself," he stated in a soft, confident voice that did funny things to her insides. "I do. Particularly since Dash Nelson has the advantage of a head start."

Noelle folded her arms in front of her. "I'm not a prize for the taking."

Undeterred, Kevin quipped, "How about a heart just waiting to be won, then?"

She huffed. "I am not going to be involved in your competition."

"Glad to hear it." Kevin wrapped his arms around her, brought her close. He threaded one hand through her hair. "I don't want to fight him for you, either. I just want you for myself."

The passion in his voice stole her breath. "Kevin…"

"Kiss me like you mean it, Noelle," he ordered, slowly bringing his lips down to hers. "And I promise I'll kiss you back the same way."

The intensity of his kiss drew forth a well of emotions she wanted to pretend didn't exist. Noelle groaned, even as she kissed him back passionately. "I knew if I kept seeing you this would happen," she admitted ruefully. They'd end up making love. She'd end up wanting more….

Kevin lifted her up so she was sitting on the counter, arms wrapped around his neck, his strong, hard body ensconced in the open V of her legs. The insides of her thighs rubbed against the outside of his. "I knew it, too," he confessed gruffly.

If only he knew everything about her. All her secrets. The pain of her past. If only she was sure he could accept the truth, should it ever come out, as she always feared it would.

Forcing herself back to the sweetness of the moment instead of the uncertainty of the future,

Noelle closed her eyes and rested her forehead on his shoulder.

"Why do you think I've been coming around so much?" He kissed the side of her neck.

Trying to keep things simple, she guessed lightly, "For sex?" She arched, her breasts brushing against his chest, as his lips targeted the sensitive place behind her ear.

"Guess again." Still driving her mad with sensation, he lifted the hem of her shirt, his hands roving higher.

She trembled as his palms molded her breasts through the smooth knit of her sports bra, his thumbs running over the tender crests. "So you won't feel so alone…at Christmastime…" she said breathlessly.

"So I can be with you," he corrected.

His eyes held hers with the promise of passionate lovemaking to come. She hadn't allowed herself to want anything for herself in such a long time. Hadn't allowed herself to hope…. Kevin McCabe was bringing back her faith.

"If I stay…" he warned softly.

"I know." She held his gaze, sure about this much. "I want you, too." Wise or not, she wanted to lose herself in the spirit of the season and feel close to someone again. She wanted the bliss—the intimacy—only Kevin could bring. Being with him like this was the only present she needed. Tangling her fingers in his hair, she wrapped her legs around his waist and brought his head back down to hers. Their lips fused in an explosion of heat and hunger, and then his tongue swept her mouth with a kiss that sent her emotions soaring. Overwhelmed by the pleasurable sensations, she returned his embrace with everything she had. Until that wasn't enough…for either of them.

His heartbeat racing in time with her own, he asked hoarsely, "Upstairs?"

Already trembling, Noelle nodded. "My bedroom."

Cupping his hands beneath her bottom, he lifted her off the counter and, with her still clasped against him, carried her easily up the stairs.

"Last room on the left," Noelle whispered

between kisses, keeping her legs locked tight about his waist, her arms about his neck, her midriff pressed to his.

Kevin set her down next to the bed, his gaze intently locked with hers. His arms tightened around her possessively and his expression showed both fierce satisfaction and wonder. Then he kissed her, hard and sweet. She felt his need and yearning, and it mirrored hers. In that endless kiss, they drew from each other—Noelle surrendering one moment, taking control the next. Helpless to resist, she arched against him, the need in her an incessant ache. Easing his hands beneath her top, to her breasts, he murmured, "You'll have to show me what you like."

What didn't she like when it came to him? Noelle wondered, breathing in the wintry fragrance of his aftershave lotion.

"How about everything," she responded, her breasts swelling and nipples beading. Aware she had never felt sexier in her life as she did when she was with him, she let the sandpapery feel of his evening beard sensually abrade her face. He bent his head, the slow strokes of his tongue across hers unbearably seductive. And still it wasn't enough, for either of them. Her shirt came over her head, her bra was unclasped, pants and panties whisked off.

"Starting with this..." Noelle continued, making short work of getting him naked, too. She ran her hands across hard muscle and smooth skin. He was absolutely beautiful. So beautiful she couldn't take her eyes from his broad shoulders, nicely sculpted chest, well-defined pecs and flat abs. And lower still... Not that she was the only one admiring. He had paused to look at her, too, his eyes taking in the soft curves of her breasts and rosy-pink nipples.

"Have I told you how gorgeous you are...?" he whispered, guiding her to sit on the edge of the bed.

He certainly made her feel gorgeous, Noelle thought, as he laid her back gently and stretched out beside her. Rolling her onto her side, he took her in his arms and kissed her again and again, until a fire roared within her and her body tingled with heat. That quickly, Noelle was ready for him, but Kevin seemed determined to take his time and make their lovemaking last. Grasping both her wrists in one hand, he anchored them above her head and held them there. He smiled at the way she trembled. Then he kissed his way down her neck, to the very tip of her breast, his lips suckling the pale pink circle and lingering there until she felt deliciously aroused. An urgency swept through her and she made soft, breathless sounds of pleasure as he turned his attention to her other breast.

Nothing had ever felt so wonderfully stimulating. Parting her legs, she moved restlessly on the bed. She was so wet and they'd barely started yet.

"Have I told you how much I'm going to enjoy making you mine?" he continued. The possessiveness in his voice sent another thrill shooting through her.

"Kevin…" she murmured as he paid homage to the underside of her breasts, the sensitive juncture between her ribs.

"I guess you like this," he observed, an expression of sheer male appreciation on his face.

She moaned. Still holding her captive, he moved lower still. "How about this?" Eyes sparkling, he dipped his tongue into the well of her navel.

She sent him a look that spoke volumes about the state of her arousal.

"And this?" He let go of her hands only to grasp her hips and start kissing her thighs. She meant to retain some element of control. It proved impossible. Her body ignited, and she was so consumed with wanting him inside her that she could barely breathe. And, to her dismay, he knew it. His gaze traveled over her, the desire in his eyes as unmistakable as the hardness of his body brushing against hers. Flush with victory, he slid a hand between her legs. "Or this…" Still smiling, he found her with his lips and hands, making her blossom, sending her to the brink.

Needing to give as well as receive, she tried to wrestle free. "Let me…touch you…." she gasped, knowing now was no time to be selfish.

Letting her know he was still the one in charge, Kevin chuckled. "In due time." He held fast, making her tremble with need. And then his mouth was on her in the most intimate of kisses, demanding total surrender.

She went. Boy, did she go. And then he was sliding up, covering her body completely with his own again. Possessing her with one smooth, sure stroke. Awash with sensation, heart brimming with unexpected love, Noelle rose up to meet him. Easing his hands beneath her, he lifted her, going deeper, slower, stronger. The essences of their bodies blended, bringing them closer still, making them one. Until there was no more thinking, only feeling this hot, melting bliss.

Chapter Ten

Reality returned with stunning speed. Noelle rolled onto her side, hardly able to believe she had lost control like that, and forced herself to sit up. What had she been thinking? Getting involved with a member of law enforcement who had a definite aversion to females with less than stellar pasts?

Kevin sat up, too, a perplexed expression on his face. "Where are you going?"

"I have to think." She disappeared into the bathroom, drew a long, bolstering breath, then returned with a robe tied tightly around her waist.

"I'm not going to say I'm sorry this happened," Kevin warned her stubbornly, every bit the take-charge detective once again.

"I'm not, either," Noelle replied, forcing herself

to meet his searching gaze with a bravado she couldn't begin to feel. "Because that would be a lie. Nor will I say that I don't want it to ever happen again. I do. But only," she stressed softly, pausing to let her words sink in, determined to do whatever necessary to be in full control of her life once again, "on my terms."

RUSHING INTO A love affair had never been Kevin's style, particularly with a woman involved—at least peripherally—in a situation he was still investigating. But what the heck. He figured the two of them were adult enough to handle it. If Noelle would let them, that was. "Is that the way it usually works with you?" he asked, feeling a deep satisfaction at being with her like this. "Everything is your way or not at all?"

Without warning, the troubled light was back in her eyes. "Now that I have a son to consider, yes."

Given Noelle's elusive nature, Kevin had half expected she would pull back from their newfound intimacy as soon as the aftershocks in their bodies faded. "And before then?" he inquired, watching as she ran a brush through her hair.

The corners of her lips lifted in a rueful smile. "I tended to want it my way, too."

"Why am I not surprised by that?"

She perched on the edge of the bed. "This was nice."

More than nice, Kevin thought. They had only been apart ten minutes, and already his body ached to possess hers again. And his heart...well, to his chagrin that was in no better shape. Figuring she would be more comfortable if he had some clothes on, too, Kevin pulled on his pants and shirt. "But?"

Noelle took a deep breath, beginning to look a little panicked as she regarded him steadily. "I'm not in the market for a relationship, other than friendship."

As a cop, Kevin had learned when a person was holding back—and Noelle was holding back plenty. But he also sensed she had revealed far more to him than she normally did.

"Like you have with Dash."

A fiery blush deepened the color in her cheeks.

She picked up Kevin's boots, handed them to him and wordlessly directed him to the upstairs hall and down the stairs. She waited until they reached the kitchen before continuing matter-of-factly, "Dash and I don't—we've never—"

Aware she was getting ready to send him on his way, Kevin stepped into his boots. "You're telling me Dash Nelson's never put the moves on you?"

Noelle blew out an exasperated breath, looking supremely irritated that he was forcing her to spell it out for him. "Once." She met his eyes forthrightly, then set about making a fresh pot of coffee. "A while ago, about six months after my husband died. It was awkward. I think we both realized it wasn't a place we wanted to go again."

"Or maybe Dash is just waiting for the right time and place." Such as Christmas Eve, Kevin thought. When Dash planned to propose marriage....

"I don't think so," she retorted. "Dash knows…"

"Knows what?" Kevin pressed, stunned by the depth of his feelings for her.

Noelle paused. "All the reasons I didn't really want to get married the first time around."

"Which were?" Kevin edged closer.

"Look," she said finally, "I'm not the person you think I am."

"Then who are you? Mata Hari?"

She gave him a chiding look. "I know what kind of woman you need in your life."

So did he, as it happened. "Someone exactly like you. Someone who loves kids." *Someone who knows how to love me.*

Distress glittered in her eyes. "You come from this big happy family where everyone knows everything about everyone else, and that's not me. I would never fit in."

Another hint that her childhood had been less than stellar, Kevin noted, his heart going out to her. "What are you trying to tell me?" he joked, covering up his hurt that she thought so little of herself and of him. "You have a criminal past?"

Noelle stepped back abruptly. "I've said everything I have to say," she said in a low, dismissive tone. "You need to leave."

KEVIN KNEW HE COULD no longer turn a blind eye—he had to check this out. Instead of heading home when he got back to Laramie, he drove to the sheriff's department. Typically quiet for 2:00 a.m. on a weeknight, the station held a scattering of deputies and support staff. Rio was there, too, sitting at his desk, typing with two fingers.

"What are you working on?" Kevin asked, checking out his computer screen.

"An accident report. Six-car fender bender across the street from the post office." Rio squinted and tilted his head. "You know how many different versions of what happened there are?"

Glad to think about someone's problems other than his own, if only for a minute, Kevin lifted a brow. "Six?"

His buddy scowled, impatient as ever with the paperwork. "Try fourteen," he fumed. "Drivers, passengers, innocent bystanders…everybody's got a different story. And they all gotta be written up." Rio kicked back in his chair. "So why are you here?"

"I've got to run a check on something," Kevin murmured, booting up his own computer. He had to find out if there had been anything to Noelle's kicked-in-the-gut reaction to his joking comment about her having a "criminal past." He had to see if there was anything attorney Dash Nelson—and Noelle—might be keeping from him.

So he went back to the first real clue that all was not as it appeared, and looked up the names of Noelle's parents. He also did a search of Texas real estate agents and property appraisers for the last ten years. Neither her mother's or father's name showed up.

He tried Idaho. And got the same result.

His heart sank. He couldn't believe Noelle had lied to him about something as basic as her parents' professions. Unless there was a mistake in the public background information he was just not picking up on. Social security numbers that had gotten altered or switched in a computer glitch. Something weird that no one knew about yet... Suddenly, Kevin became aware that Rio was standing next to him, his hand on Kevin's shoulder.

"Let's go outside and have a smoke," Rio said.

Kevin frowned at his friend. "You don't smoke."

"Neither do you." He flashed an ornery grin. "But I don't see why that should stop us."

Outside in the bracing night air, Kevin glanced at the evergreen wreaths decorating every street-lamp in the historic downtown area, as well as the glittering lights of the huge Christmas tree on the lawn of city hall. Rio obviously didn't care about the scenery. He got out a pack of gum and handed Kevin a piece. "You've been spending a lot of time with Noelle Kringle and her son. You hooking up with her or what?"

Kevin wished he knew. His gut told him that she was trying to keep him at arm's length as much for his sake as hers. Her actions were as puzzling as they were frustrating. He glared at his col-league. "Since when have you ever known me to answer questions about my personal life?"

Rio shrugged and turned the collar of his jacket up against the cold. "Since never. Of course, after what happened with Portia, I didn't think you'd ever trust a woman you just met again, either."

That was the problem, Kevin thought. He totally trusted Noelle, despite the mounting signs that said he should be a lot more cautious. "If you must know, she and I've had one date." *And made love one time.* Aware his friend wanted more info than that, Kevin added in his most disinterested tone, "She seems like a nice lady."

Rio studied him. "Probably just trying to make up for that citizen's arrest."

"Or working up to doing it again," he quipped.

Rio's smile faded. "Stop evading, buddy. Tell me what's going on."

Kevin knew he was far from objective. He needed a sounding board. Rio would provide it. Kevin explained the discrepancies between the information in the background check and what Noelle had told him.

The deputy shrugged. "So maybe Noelle wasn't brought up by her parents. Maybe she got dumped on the doorstep of her godparents, or an aunt and uncle, or even a couple of family friends, and considers them her folks. Or lived with a variety of relatives over the years. You know, fifth grade with Aunt Matilda, sixth grade with Gramma, seventh with Tom and Sally and their three kids. That would explain the different locations. You and I both know it happens."

"Then why wouldn't she have said so?" he argued tensely.

"Because she's embarrassed, that's why. Who wants to admit your parents didn't really want or love you? Or that maybe nobody else really did, either."

Normally, Kevin could sort through this, but his emotions were clouding his ability to analyze and examine the facts. He fell silent, thinking. "And maybe I'm just not seeing what's right in front of me because I'm..." falling for her, he almost said out loud "...dazzled by her beauty," he finished finally.

"Understandable," Rio concurred, as a lone car drove past them. "Except you never struck me as a guy who got led around by his johnson. You are, however, a guy who really likes a good chase. And from what I hear from Miss Sadie and the other ladies over at Laramie Gardens Home for Seniors, you've got quite a challenge, winning that gal's heart, 'cause she's as elusive as the day is long."

Kevin leaned against the building. The coldness of the brick seeped through his clothing and he shoved his hands in his pockets. "Thanks for the vote of confidence."

"Just telling it like it is." Rio sobered. "Look, my advice remains the same. If you don't want to come right out and ask her why there are discrepancies—"

"Oh, that'll go over well," Kevin predicted sarcastically. "'By the way, Noelle, I've been snooping and guess what? I suspect you're a damn liar. And a pretty bad one at that.'"

Rio rubbed his jaw. "I can see where that might ruin a budding romance," he said dryly.

As well as both of their Christmases. "Gee. You think?"

"Particularly," Rio deduced compassionately, "if she's just starting to broach a subject that is very painful."

Kevin frowned. What if Noelle *was* the victim of some sort of neglect or abuse? What if those actions had led to someone's arrest, just not hers? Was it possible that was the secret behind her skittishness? "So what are you suggesting I do?" he demanded gruffly.

"Keep searching for the truth," Rio advised. "'Cause knowing you, you're not going to rest until you know why Noelle's story and the facts you found on record do not match up."

Figuring Rio was right and knowing Noelle might not ever be willing to open up enough to tell him the truth about what could have been a very devastating childhood, Kevin made a phone call to a friend in Houston early the next morning.

"Hey, Alicia," he said, when he got her on the line. "How's the P.I. business?"

"Busy, as always," Alicia Allen replied. "What can I do for you, McCabe?"

"That favor you owe me from our police academy days?" Kevin replied. "I'm collecting."

NOELLE HAD WANTED to call Kevin all day and make amends for the way their previous evening together had ended. As she drove back to Laramie and settled down to work on the upcoming Blue Santa party, she'd found herself waiting for her cell phone to ring. Which irritated her all the more. She didn't want to get emotionally involved with him, yet her heart was already involved, and she didn't know what she was going to do about that.

Those feelings escalated when she looked up and saw Kevin McCabe stride in to the community center, in a denim shirt, jeans and boots, clearly ready to get down to work, too. Feeling her cheeks heat at the memory of what they had done, Noelle ducked around a ladder and headed for the door to the kitchen.

"Well, look who's standing under the mistletoe," Rio Vasquez remarked.

Three of the single off-duty deputies stopped hanging garlands, glanced over and grinned. Before anyone else could get there, Kevin McCabe stepped in. Noelle gave him a look that said, *Don't You Dare*. Predictably, Kevin kept right on coming. The next thing she knew he had his hands linked around her waist. "You can't really be thinking of kissing me here," Noelle murmured.

"Actually," he said, bending her backward from the waist, lowering his head to hers and looking very much like a man in love, "I think I am."

She barely had time to gasp before his hand was threading through her hair and his lips were moving on hers with the passion she had yearned to know again.

She meant to resist him, but there was just something about the way he kissed her, so provocatively and surely, that totally sapped her resolve. He was so masculine and confident, so determined and giving. She reveled in the teasing sweep of his tongue and the hard demand of his tall, strong body, knowing that even before the sweet embrace ended, news of their romance would be all over town. Heck, given the McCabe connections, all over the state...

Kevin knew he was putting his reputation as a law enforcement officer on the line, staking his claim to Noelle this way. He couldn't help it. Walking in and seeing her looking so very beautiful had set his heart to racing. The glance she had thrown him—half challenge, half yearning—had sealed the deal. Knowing she was every bit as unsettled and confused as he was about the passion between them told him her feelings were genuine.

He had been without true devotion for far too long to let it go easily now. And she did care for him, he thought, as she made a soft helpless sound of pleasure deep in her throat and kissed him back. Luxuriating in the clean, fragrant scent of her, he shifted her even closer. Only the soft murmur of laughter and a few teasing catcalls had them pulling apart once again.

Kevin looked up to see Rio watching. His fellow cop shook his head as if to say, *You've got it bad, buddy.*

Don't I know that, Kevin thought. To break the ice and lighten the speculation, he looked back at Noelle. "Are we going to stand around here kissing all day or are we going to get some work done?" he joked.

Blushing, she said, "I'm going back to work. You need to *get* to work."

More laughter followed.

Noelle strode off. From a table in the corner, she

picked up a clipboard and pen, and went back to telling some of the other deputies how she wanted decorations positioned.

Will McCabe strode toward Kevin, carrying an armload of wreaths and garlands. "Looks like you made up your mind whether or not to get involved with her," he murmured in a low voice.

Kevin guessed he had. He walked back out to Will's pickup to help bring in the rest of the greenery. "I could lose in this situation so many ways," he confided to his older brother.

Will gave him a sympathetic look that said he had known his own share of heartaches, via a rocky marriage and divorce. "Because of Dash Nelson?"

Kevin nodded, aware Will had vowed never to marry again. "Dash is planning to ask Noelle to marry him on Christmas Eve, probably in the midst of some big party he's throwing for Miss Sadie."

"Which puts the pressure on Noelle to say yes," Will guessed.

Kevin loaded up his arms with fragrant smelling pine boughs trimmed with red ribbon. "Not that she necessarily would."

"But she might," Will said.

Kevin exhaled, offered a tight nod. He hadn't realized until now how much that possibility scared him.

Will took out as much as he could carry, then closed the tailgate with his foot. "You still want to be in the game?"

Kevin shot his brother a dry look. "What do you think?"

Together, they ambled toward the community center door. "Does she know how interested you are?"

"I think that kiss spoke for itself," Kevin responded as they walked across the parking lot.

"Maybe." Will narrowed his gaze. "And maybe she just thinks you were showing off because you had an audience."

If any guy would see trouble with a woman coming, it was Will, who'd undergone more than one trial by fire with his faithless ex. "So your advice is?" Kevin asked, aware his heart was suddenly pounding at the thought of all that was on the line.

Will smiled. "I say you only live once. If this is what you want for Christmas, go for it."

"NOELLE?" Laney McCabe emerged from the community center nursery with Mikey in her arms. Brad McCabe's wife was as affable as she was pretty. Her skills as a devoted mother of three had put her in charge of the children who had tagged along with their parents doing the prep work for the party. "I think you better come here."

Noelle put down the red velvet ribbon she'd been about to hang and hurried over to Kevin's sister-in-law. "What is it?"

Laney frowned in concern. "Mikey feels awfully warm to me."

He looked unusually flushed, too, Noelle noted. She pressed her hand to his cheek. "Oh, dear."

Laney bit her lip. "You think he might be running a fever?"

Noelle nodded. When Kevin joined them, she turned to him. "I think Mikey's getting sick. And my pediatrician is in Houston."

Kevin plucked the cell phone from the leather

holder on his belt. "Want me to call my brother Riley? He's a family doc as well as Miss Sadie's physician here."

"If you wouldn't mind…" Noelle said in relief.

Laney excused herself to go back to the nursery, while Kevin made the inquiry. "Riley's over at the E.R.," he said, after hanging up. "If we want to meet him at the hospital he'll see Mikey right away."

For her son's sake, Noelle did her best to maintain a casual attitude on the way to the hospital. It wasn't easy, given the wealth of emotions roiling around inside her.

"Are *you* feeling all right?" Kevin asked, once they'd been shown to an exam room.

Noelle flushed. She should have known the wily detective wouldn't miss a thing. "Yes, of course," she answered promptly.

He touched her face with the back of his hand and frowned. "I think you might be spiking a fever, too."

She squared her shoulders. "Don't be ridiculous. I never get sick."

Before either of them could say more, the door

opened. Riley McCabe and his wife, nurse Amanda Witherspoon McCabe, came in. "I think you should take Noelle's temperature, too," Kevin said.

Oh, for heaven's sake! "It's not necessary," she told them flatly.

Both medical professionals gave Noelle a close look, then exchanged glances. "A wicked twenty-four hour virus is going around," Riley said.

Amanda popped a thermometer in Noelle's mouth. "It's very contagious. All of our kids have had it. And Laurel and her husband, Cade, had something similar, back in Dallas, several weeks ago."

Noelle removed the thermometer long enough to ask, "Did you get it?"

Riley turned on the light in his otoscope. "Amanda did. I didn't."

"Don't get him started on the survival of the fittest." Amanda gently eased one of Mikey's arms out of the sleeve of his shirt and took his temperature under it. Riley listened to his chest, checked his ears, throat and nose, then did the same for Noelle, while Kevin held Mikey. "We're going to run a blood test to be sure, but it looks like the virus."

Noelle went first, demonstrating that the quick, nearly painless procedure was no big deal. To no avail. Mikey burst into tears and wailed loudly when Amanda took the blood sample, which made Noelle cry. Kevin's eyes were suspiciously moist, too, as he put his arm around the two of them.

"I can't stand to see him hurting." Noelle whispered as she continued to comfort her son as best she could.

"I know. I feel the same way." He eased Noelle back onto the gurney with Mikey on her lap, then perched beside them. The three of them cuddled together. Now that his indignation had been expressed, Mikey looked as if he would fall asleep then and there.

Amanda popped back in with the paperwork and written instructions. "Do you have someone to stay with the two of you?" she asked Noelle.

Kevin spoke up. "They have me."

USED TO COPING ON HER OWN in situations like this, Noelle had to admit it was nice to be able to lean on Kevin's very strong shoulder. "Thanks for doing this," she told him sincerely, two hours later.

He smiled and reached over to squeeze her hand. "I'm glad to help."

He'd done more than that. He'd driven her van, so she could sit in back with Mikey. He'd stopped at the supermarket and run in to get grocery essentials and acetaminophen. Once back at Blackberry Hill, he'd helped her get some soup and juice into Mikey and prepare him for bed. Then he insisted she get into her pajamas, too.

Kevin watched her cradle her sleeping son to her chest, rocking him gently. "Do you think we should take Mikey's temperature again?" he murmured quietly.

Reluctantly, Noelle got up and carried the boy to his portable crib. Gently, she eased him down into it and covered him with a blanket. "No," she whispered, giving Mikey one last look before switching on the baby monitor and backing out of the bedroom. "We'd have to wake him, and we just took it thirty minutes ago. He doesn't feel any warmer."

Kevin grasped her hand in his as they walked down the hall.

Noelle fought the familiar panic building inside her. "I just wish he wasn't sick." Although she wanted to hover, she made herself go back down the stairs. She turned on the baby monitor and sank down on the sofa.

Kevin sat beside her and stretched his long legs out in front of him. "I wish both of you had managed to avoid this virus. But if you had to get it, better now than on Christmas, right?"

Noelle avoided his searching gaze. "I guess," she murmured. Curious, she studied him. "Aren't you afraid you'll get it?" As good as Dash was to her—and he had been wonderful—he never really wanted to be around when either she or Mikey had anything the least bit contagious.

"No. Viruses don't scare me." Kevin stood and went into the kitchen. He returned with a glass of pineapple-orange juice for her. "The question is why are you so unnerved?" he asked, his fingers brushings hers warmly. Noelle took an enervating sip of the icy liquid, felt it soothe her parched throat. "Is this the first time Mikey's been ill?"

"No." Noelle studied the blinking lights of the Christmas tree. "He's had an ear infection and a couple of colds. A mild stomach flu once."

Kevin stroked the inside of her arm, from wrist to elbow. "And yet you're about an inch away from total panic."

She took another sip of juice. "Shows, huh?"

He nodded, interest simmering in his brown eyes.

"You're not going to let this go, are you?" she asked.

"I am a detective." His lips curled in a self-assured smile. "Every instinct I have tells me more is going on here than you've alluded to thus far."

Noelle needed to unburden herself. Gut instinct told her Kevin would understand, if she gave him half a chance. "I panic because of the way I lost my husband," she admitted sadly, swallowing around the growing knot of emotion in her throat. "He was young and healthy, too, and he came down with what we thought was the flu. Only instead of getting better after a few days, he got worse. He started having trouble catching his breath." She continued in a low, halting voice, "I had to take him to the E.R. The virus entered his lungs and then his heart. Two days later, I was a widow."

Concern sharpened the edges of Kevin's handsome face. "You must have been devastated," he said.

Noelle nodded. "Not long after that I discovered I was pregnant with Mikey. And that helped ease my grief."

Still, it had been a tough road, recovering from the tragedy.

There were times when she still felt extremely vulnerable and more than a little unsure of herself. Times when she wondered whether, if only she had gotten her husband to the hospital a few hours sooner, he would have survived. Times when she knew that his fate was not in her hands at all.

Part of Kevin wished they had never started this conversation. His inquisitive side needed to know whether or not he was competing with a ghost. Because that was one contest he was fairly certain would be darn near impossible to win. He took her hand in his. "Do you still miss Michael?"

"I miss what we might have had."

"Dash thinks you might be ready to start dating again."

"Dash didn't say that!" Noelle exclaimed in a way that made Kevin want to haul her into his arms and kiss her until she melted against him, virus or no.

"How do you know?" he taunted playfully, edging closer.

"Because Dash knows I'm not a dating person," Noelle said. "I'm a relationship person."

So was Kevin. "What's the difference?" he challenged.

"Some women like to go out a lot—casually—whether they're really interested in a guy or not," she declared indignantly, her gaze still trained stubbornly on his.

"Ah, yes," he drawled, warming to the topic. "The old SWMP."

Noelle blinked. "SWMP?"

"Single Women's Meal Plan."

She laughed. "I don't subscribe to that."

"Then allow me to rephrase. Have you had a relationship with anyone else since you've been a widow?"

Noelle huffed. "Please. I haven't even kissed anyone."

"Until me," Kevin concluded.

"Yes, well..." she waved dismissively "...you're an exception in a lot of ways."

He knew she wanted him to think so. Just as she wanted him to think all they had going for them was a holiday affair. He flashed her a wry grin. "Because I look so much like a trespassing bum?"

Merriment sparkled in Noelle's eyes. "You're never going to let me live that down, are you?"

"It was a memorable day," he countered affably. "First time I've ever been called Santa or chased by a woman brandishing a large plastic candy cane."

Noelle wrinkled her nose. "I didn't chase you."

"Would you?"

She tilted her head thoughtfully, warming to

the flirting going on between them. "I thought you were the one doing the chasing."

And he'd keep it up as long as she continued to enjoy it. "I just might be in hot pursuit," he allowed softly. *Very* hot pursuit.

Noelle nibbled on her lip, the wariness suddenly back in her eyes. "The question is why."

"Because I've never met a woman like you, that's why."

Chapter Eleven

Kevin was trying so hard to be gallant. Not that Noelle was making it easy for him. "I don't want to go to bed," she protested as he steered her into her room. Frilly lavender bedding dominated the antique mahogany four-poster. The canopy was similarly decked out. "I'm not sleepy," she protested when he relieved her of her thick terry-cloth bathrobe and slippers and urged her beneath the covers.

"Shh." Kevin pressed a finger to her lips. "You'll wake the baby."

Noelle sighed and settled against the pillows. Her cheeks were flushed, her eyes fever-bright. Her temp had risen to 101.9 in the last half hour. He didn't want it to go any higher, and figured the best way to prevent it was by getting her to sleep as soon as possible.

Humor laced her voice. "You're awfully bossy."

Kevin reminded himself he was a McCabe, and McCabes were chivalrous to the core. "I'm the medic in charge."

She took a moment to scowl at him. "You just don't want me talking anymore."

Heaven help him, he wanted to make love to her here and now. He grinned. "You're right, I don't."

She studied him, a new softness in her gaze. "How come?"

Tenderness swept through him. Kevin brought the covers up across her chest and tucked them in around her. Finished, he rested a palm on either side of her. Ignoring the persistent need to kiss her, he leaned in to confide gently, "Because you, like me, are one of those people who become hyper— rather than lethargic—when they have a fever."

He had seen it a lot on emergency calls. A patient who should have been passed out with a high fever was instead running around at high speed, doing something ridiculous, insisting he or she was fine. Often to the chagrin of the loved one who had dialed 9-1-1.

Mischief played at the corners of her lips. "So I'm a little hyper. So what?"

"So that acetaminophen you just took is going to have a better chance of working if you're quiet," Kevin declared sternly.

Noelle scoffed. "You don't know that."

"Well, I'm going to pretend I do. Seriously." He paused, suddenly as reluctant to say good-night as she was. "Do you have everything you need?"

Except you. In bed. With me, her expression said. "I guess," she murmured finally.

Wishing he could climb under the covers with her, Kevin kissed the top of her head. "I'll be across the hall if you need anything."

"Okay." Noelle caught his hand, held it tightly. "Thanks for everything, Detective."

"You're welcome." He touched the side of her face, not sure when he had ever felt such overwhelming devotion. Rio was right. He did have it bad. He leaned forward and kissed her temple. "Get some sleep."

NOELLE OPENED HER EYES to sunlight sifting through the curtains.

Kevin was stretched out beside her, cuddling Mikey against his chest. Another blink of her eyes had her noting that Kevin was on top of the bedcovers. She was beneath them. Fuzzy memories of him helping her through the night filtered back.

She eased from the bed. Although she still felt a little dizzy and weak, she was definitely more clearheaded. Heading for the bathroom, Noelle splashed cold water on her face and brushed her teeth. She tugged a brush through her hair before padding back into the bedroom.

Kevin's eyes were open, watching her as she pulled on her thick terry robe and slippers. Mikey stirred sleepily on his chest, near waking, too.

Surprised by the emotions shifting through her, Noelle curled up on the bed beside them. If she had been attracted to Kevin before, it was nothing to how she felt now, after a night of his almost unbearable kindness. This, she mused, was what a close intimate relationship should be like in times of crisis. Not what she'd had before—in her family, in her marriage—with each person tending to his or her own needs first and foremost before helping the other. Kevin had put her and Mikey ahead of everything else. It felt good to be the recipient of such loving care.

"How are you feeling?" he asked, his voice a sexy rumble.

Noelle favored him with a smile, the gratitude she felt nothing compared to the desire simmering deep inside her. "Like the morning after a wild party. Only there was no party."

He chuckled and stretched as well as he could without disturbing her son. "How much of last night do you remember?"

Noelle paused to reflect. "You kept waking me up to take my temperature."

Kevin nodded. "Every four hours—for both of you."

Remembering the tenderness of his touch, she bit her lip. "You made me drink something and gave me acetaminophen."

"And did the same for Mikey."

Speaking of whom… Noelle reached over and felt her drowsy son's forehead. It felt normal to the touch. Or maybe her hand was extra warm; she couldn't tell. Fortunately, Kevin already had the baby thermometer in his hand. Knowing it would be easier to do this before Mikey woke up all the way, Noelle shifted him gently and eased his arm from his pajama top. Kevin slid the thermometer underneath. Their eyes met as they waited for the results.

More memories drifted back, sexy, unbidden. Noelle moaned softly. "Tell me I didn't…"

He quirked a brow. "Come onto me?"

Embarrassment heated her cheeks. "Okay, that was blunt."

"Yeah, you did," he told her, obviously pleased. "But I was a complete gentleman."

"Thank heaven." Noelle waved off the erotic thoughts.

"In deed, anyway," Kevin continued rakishly. "My thoughts were a little more fanciful."

She tried to make light of that as their eyes met. "Mmm-hmming me in your mind?" She mimicked his teasing tone.

Kevin sobered. "More like my heart."

Okay, that was romantic. More so because he looked every bit as surprised by the words he had just murmured as she was. Noelle reached out to check Kevin's forehead. "Funny," she said, "I could have sworn you were delirious."

"No. That was you," he stated, over the beep of the digital thermometer. "And speaking of body heat, your palm feels awfully warm."

Noelle waited for him to withdraw the thermometer from beneath Mikey's arm, then readjusted her son's pajama top. "What's his temp?"

"Ninety-nine point two."

She sighed in relief. That probably meant he was on the mend.

"Now let's take yours." Kevin popped a thermometer under her tongue, shifted her stirring son to her arms and then headed off. He returned with a box of baby wipes and a clean diaper for Mikey. "You going to let me change you, big guy?" he asked, noting the toddler's eyes were open now and he was looking around.

Mikey broke out in a big grin. "Sleep!" He grabbed Kevin's shirt and Noelle's pajama top. "We sleep!"

"Yes. We all slept together last night." Kevin started changing Mikey's diaper like a pro. "'Cause you wanted to be held and Mommy wanted you in her sight at all times."

How easy it would be to depend on this, on him. Which was why, Noelle thought pensively, she should put on the brakes. She went to get toddler-size corduroy pants, a sweater and socks. "Shouldn't you be at work?" She helped Mikey into his day clothes.

Kevin slipped the soggy diaper into a plastic disposal bag. "I let the department know last night I was taking a personal day to take care of a sick friend." He walked into the bathroom to wash his hands.

Noelle passed her son a miniature fire truck. "So it's going to be all over town you were out here with me all night?"

Kevin smiled, watching Mikey run the vehicle over the rumpled covers. "People understand the situation. And for anyone who doesn't, who cares?" He sat on the side of the bed. Taking her hand, he pulled her down beside him. "Why? Does that bother you?"

Noting Mikey was a little too close to the edge, Noelle caught him and returned him to the middle. "I don't like being the center of negative attention."

Kevin smiled. "It's true, when you're trying something new, the fewer people who know about it, the better."

She had to wait for her heartbeat to return to normal. "Are we trying something new here?"

He gave her a look more potent than any kiss. "What do you think?"

KEVIN'S PAGER WENT OFF just as he and Noelle were talking about what to have for dinner that evening. It had been a really nice day. He had enjoyed hanging out with her and Mikey, caring for them while they took it easy, as per his brother

Riley's orders. It figured the day would end with an interruption he couldn't ignore.

"Important?" Noelle asked.

"Probably," Kevin replied, reaching for the phone. Otherwise, the sheriff's department would not have summoned him.

Rio Vasquez quickly brought Kevin up to speed. "A young kid's here, asking to see you. Sixteen or so. Long hair. Really nice clothes, part of which might be some sort of private school uniform. Looks like a runaway. He said he's the son of an old friend of yours. But I'm not buying it. In fact, I think he might be in some kind of trouble. Said his name is Harry Smith."

"Not too original."

"At least it wasn't Jones," Rio quipped, referring to the two most commonly used aliases. "Can you get in here?"

"In about thirty to forty minutes. Can you stall him that long?"

"No problem. I'll distract him with the Christmas cookies in the coffee room."

"So what's going on?" Noelle asked curiously when Kevin hung up the phone.

"There's a kid answering Scooter Roth's description over at the sheriff's department who says he won't talk to anyone but me."

"Then you should go."

"I'm planning to, but only if you and Mikey agree to come into town with me. I can drop you at my house before heading over to the station."

Noelle wrinkled her nose, perplexed. "And this is necessary because…?"

"You're both still running low-grade fevers."

"Ninety-nine point five," Noelle retorted cheerfully. "That's barely above normal."

Kevin didn't care if he sounded like a worried old woman—he wasn't taking any chances. "It's still only late afternoon. Your temperatures could both spike again, and I don't like the idea of you and Mikey being so far from me if that happens." He didn't want them away from him, period, if they were sick. "Besides, you haven't had dinner yet. Seriously, I'll feel better if you're nearby. You and Mikey can spend the night there in my fully equipped guest suite. You'd even have your own bathroom."

"I'm going." Noelle quickly gathered up the things needed for an overnight stay, setting them in the front hall. "But only because I want you to talk to Scooter Roth before he loses his nerve, and I have the feeling this is the only way to accomplish that."

Unfortunately, Kevin thought so, too. But as soon as his session with the kid was over he was heading back to Noelle and Mikey.

THE TEENAGER STOOD when Kevin entered the coffee room. The cookie plate in front of him was empty. He didn't appear to have had a shower since Kevin had last seen him, and his clothes looked as if they had been slept in. He swallowed nervously. "I don't know if you remember me…."

"Scooter Roth, right?"

"Yeah." Scooter paused, looking sheepish. "About the name I gave Deputy Vasquez…I wasn't sure I should even be here, and I didn't know where else to find you."

Kevin sized the youth up, realized he was still about to bolt. "You did good, kid. I'm glad you came." He looked over to see the Mac Callahan's Pizza delivery guy standing in the doorway, a stack of pizzas in hand. Kevin motioned the man over and pulled out a couple of bills. He paid him, set three of the boxes on a desk. "Three for them, one for us." Kevin winked. With his hand on Scooter's shoulder, he led the way back to an interrogation room and set the box on the table.

"Want a soda to go with that?" Kevin opened the box and shoved it toward Scooter.

He nodded. "Lemon lime. Please."

Kevin returned with two cold drinks and sat across from him. While Scooter downed three-quarters of the pepperoni pie, Kevin ate a slice and chatted about the upcoming basketball season and football bowl games. For someone alleged to be in debt to a cyber bookie, Scooter was amazingly uninformed about the prospects of the various teams. "Your parents know you left Houston to drive to Laramie?" Kevin asked eventually.

Scooter tensed. "How'd you know I drove?"

"Generally speaking, not too many cars with Houston private school stickers get parked across the street."

"Oh."

Kevin shrugged. "I'm just wondering why they wouldn't know. They're going all-out to help you with this jam you're in, and everything."

"Yeah, well…" Scooter played with a piece of crust.

"Could it be," Kevin said, following a hunch, "your folks really don't want to see you get out of this mess—at least to the point you escape the blame?"

Scooter swallowed hard. His face turned pale and he dropped the last of his pizza. "Why does it matter to you whether I take the rap or not?" he asked.

Kevin shrugged and sat back in his chair. "Because I think you're a good kid who's been in a bad situation. And I think you're scared."

The stubborn expression was back on Scooter's face. "My folks say I don't need to be."

Kevin tilted his head, considering. "That lawyer you have has been known to work a few miracles in cases where reasonable doubt exists, not where kids are caught committing a crime red-handed. The D.A. has videotape surveillance footage, fingerprints, your log-in on the computer, eyewitnesses, an e-mail trail. You're not getting off." He paused deliberately, letting his words sink in. "And I suspect you know that, which is why you're so scared. And that's smart. If I were you I'd hate to be taking the rap for something I didn't engineer. And I'd hate to be slapped with a heavy sentence, my future ruined by a felony conviction, while the real culprit goes free to engineer even more identity fraud."

"But I'm a juvenile," Scooter reminded him hopefully.

Kevin crushed his dreams of little penalty. "The D.A. has already petitioned the court to have you tried as an adult."

The teenager furrowed his brow. "My attorney still thinks he can get me off on a plea bargain, with community service."

"You know what I think?" Kevin asked.

Looking nervous, Scooter shook his head.

Kevin frowned. "I think—given the millions of dollars of fraudulent purchases involved—that you might find yourself wearing an orange jumpsuit sooner than anyone thinks. And I think your parents know that. And yet they still feel it's an acceptable risk to take with your future." Kevin continued his fishing expedition carefully. "And that makes me wonder if just maybe they're protecting someone else. Someone they love—or fear—more than you."

Scooter's jaw set. "My parents aren't afraid of anyone or anything."

Kevin lifted a brow, pretending he already knew all. "Even you?"

"Hey, I never implicated them!" Scooter said, in a total panic.

Suddenly, the pieces fit. "I think," Kevin murmured slowly, "you just did."

"YOU MUST BE Noelle Kringle," the gorgeous brunette said from the other side of Kevin's front door. Clad in a red chenille sweater and black pants, she carried a plastic container of soup and a basket of cranberry-orange muffins.

Noelle smiled. "And you're...?"

"His baby sister, Laurel Dunnigan. I heard you were sick and thought I'd drop off some food for him to take to you. I didn't think you and your son would be here, but I'm glad you are."

Noelle cast a glance at Mikey, sleeping in a darkened corner of the living room. She motioned Laurel into the kitchen. "Do you live in town?"

"Dallas. My husband, Cade, and I are in town to see family and give a Dunnigan Dog Food service award to the sheriff's department police dogs and their handlers."

"When is that going to happen?"

"At the community center, during the Blue Santa festivities."

Noelle removed the lid. The aroma of chicken tortilla soup wafted up, enticing her taste buds. "This soup smells delicious."

"Grandmother Lilah McCabe's recipe. Guaranteed to cure what ails you."

"Would you like some?"

Laurel chuckled. "I think I did enough tasting while I was cooking it, but I'd be happy to heat you some in the microwave and keep you company while you eat it."

Noting that Laurel seemed to know her way around her brother's kitchen better than she did, Noelle nodded. "Thanks. I met all four of your and Kevin's brothers—they helped rebuild the steps at Blackberry Hill." It was nice to meet his only sister as well, she decided, perching on a stool at the breakfast bar. "You McCabes seem like a close-knit clan."

"Yes, we are." Laurel ladled a serving of soup into a bowl. "And we're all glad Kevin is dating seriously again, too."

This was news. Noelle said casually, "That hasn't been the case?"

Laurel's expression turned rueful as she slid the soup into the microwave. "Not since he and Portia broke up and he had to leave the HPD and sort through all that mess," she said.

Just then the back door opened and closed, and Kevin walked in from the mudroom. He was carrying yet another sack of sad-looking donated baby dolls. Noelle could tell by the bits and pieces sticking out the top. "We don't need to bore Noelle with that." He gave his sister a quelling look.

Laurel sent him a glance that said she disagreed. Then she stood and smiled. "I better go." She briefly hugged her big brother. "See you tomorrow night?"

When Kevin nodded, she turned to Noelle. "I hope you feel better soon."

"Thanks." Noelle smiled. After the door shut behind Laurel, Noelle turned back to Kevin. His cheeks and nose were ruddy from the cold. His jaw bore the beginnings of an evening beard. He looked handsome and sexy, and she was ridiculously glad to see him. Even though he appeared highly annoyed at the moment. "Your sister seems nice."

The creases on either side of Kevin's mouth deepened. "She was over here, scoping out the situation for the rest of the family." The microwave dinged. He lifted out the bowl of soup and brought it to Noelle.

She tested the waters further. "They're all glad you're dating seriously again."

Kevin's eyes lit up. "So am I."

Noelle hadn't expected such a frank admission. She knew she had questions to ask. "So," she said supercasually, "who is Portia and why did you have to leave the HPD?"

He handed her a spoon and a packet of saltine crackers. "I didn't have to leave the Houston Police Department," he said. He carried over the sack of toys and set it down on the counter. "I chose to go."

Aware that her heart had begun to race, as much from the subject matter as his physical nearness, Noelle watched him squirt dish soap in the sink and add hot water. She forced herself to ask the hard questions, even though the most vulnerable part of her would almost have preferred not to know. "Why?"

Kevin rolled up his sleeves and got out a scrubber sponge from beneath the sink. He paused to give her a gruff look. "Because my career derailed after it became clear that the woman I was engaged to was an accomplished con artist, wanted in five states on a variety of felony charges," he said, immersing the first doll beneath the bubbles.

Ignoring Noelle's dismayed reaction, he began to scrub away the grime with a vengeance. "As soon as I found out Portia was living under an alias, I turned her in, but the damage to my rep was done. It didn't matter that she hadn't been actively involved in any criminal activity while she was with me, and in fact, according to her, had been trying to 'go straight.'" Kevin rinsed the doll clean. "I was the laughingstock of the department, and my credentials as detective were under fire, too."

Telling herself that thanks to the "deal" she had made, Kevin and his coworkers need never know what kind of trouble she had once been in, Noelle got a dish towel out of the drawer. Leaving her half-finished soup on the counter, she accepted the dripping toy from Kevin and began to dry it. "What happened to Portia?" she asked quietly, way too aware of the heat emanating from his much larger frame.

Kevin plucked another doll from the bag.

"She's doing time in Nevada for mail fraud and embezzlement."

Noelle's heart fluttered in her chest. "Are you over her?" She could have kicked herself the moment her words were out. Unfortunately, it was too late to take them back. *Or,* she thought to herself, *is that the reason you've been reluctant to "seriously date" since then—because you're still in love with Portia?*

Kevin turned, his demeanor grim. Gripping her shoulders, he looked down at Noelle and stated flatly, "I was over Portia the moment I found out who—and what—she was."

Would he be over her, too, Noelle wondered uncertainly, if he ever found out the whole truth? More to the point, how could she keep the details of her past from him if they were to continue getting closer? It was hard enough as it was. Carefully measuring her words. Trying to reveal only the facts of her life as it was now, as opposed to what it had really been.

Mistaking the reason behind her unease, Kevin drew her closer yet. "I can see you don't believe me," he murmured. He tucked a stray lock of her hair behind her ear. Then he rubbed his thumb across her lower lip. "So I guess I'll have to show you."

Giving her no chance to protest, he lowered his mouth to hers, used the gentle pressure of his lips to force hers apart. Unable to resist, Noelle wrapped her arms around his neck, pressed her breasts against the hardness of his chest. Desire pooled in the pit of her stomach, and her knees grew weak.

Reluctantly, Kevin drew back and broke their prolonged kiss. "I don't think… You still have fever…."

"This will make me feel better." She kept her gaze locked with his even as her heart raced in her chest.

A worried light came into his eyes. "I don't think—"

"I do." Noelle went up on tiptoe. Stifling his protest, she kissed him back with all the wonder and affection she had in her heart. He felt so good against her, so warm and sexy and male. Need sprang up deep inside her as their tongues tangled, searching, tasting, giving, taking. Noelle heard herself whimper, and then instinct and desire took over. She let herself go. Let herself surrender to the inevitable. And why not? It was Christmastime, after all. This was the only gift she wanted, her gift to herself. And to him.

Kevin knew he shouldn't be making love to her tonight, but he couldn't turn away, not when she looked at him that way, so vulnerable, so full of yearning. Not when she seemed to need him to demonstrate his emotions. What they were feeling wasn't at all convenient. But then, he thought, as he caught her beneath the knees, swung her up into his arms and headed for his bedroom, love—real love—never was.

"I gather this means you've seen the wisdom of my ways?" Noelle teased as he set her gently down beside the bed.

"You gather right." Kevin grinned. "As long as you don't get a chill." He eased her out of the trendy black warm-ups she'd been wearing, then urged her beneath the covers while he stripped down to his skin.

Knowing he wanted Noelle as he had never

wanted any woman before, he joined her beneath the blankets.

She rolled onto her side. "Somehow I feel at a disadvantage," she murmured when he took her in his arms.

"I don't know." He drew back to survey her sweat socks, pink racer-back undershirt and black bikini panties, glad she hadn't insisted he turn off the lights. "I think you look kind of cute. But if you absolutely insist on being as naked as me…"

She kissed him again. "I really do."

"Then we'll see what we can do to accommodate you," he promised hoarsely, his palms slipping up and down her spine, across her shoulders, down her arms. Blood rushed to his groin as he reveled in the silkiness of her skin. He kissed her the way he had wanted to the moment he had walked in the door that evening. Her mouth pliant beneath his, she wreathed her arms around his neck and arched against him. Loving the way she responded to him, the way she trembled when they were about to make love, Kevin put everything he had into the kiss. He was

determined this time would be every bit as satis-
fying as their first lovemaking. Even more so.
And that meant not letting her impatience, or the
soft, helpless sounds she was making in the back
of her throat, deter him.

"You'll be naked," he told her, raining kisses
down her neck, across her collarbone and the uppermost swells of her breasts, "in good time."

She hitched in a breath as he slipped his hands
beneath her camisole, cupped her breasts in his
palms. Need sprang up inside him. He pushed the
cloth higher, baring her breasts. Lifting the
softness to his mouth, he stroked the nipples with
the pads of his thumbs, then laved them with his
tongue. "Next thing I know," she complained
breathlessly, quivering with sensation, "you'll be
telling me good things come to those who wait."

"Because they do." He divested her of her top,
then slid lower, hooking his fingers in the elastic
waistband of her panties and dragging them down
over her abdomen, to the top of her thighs.

"Kevin." She caught his head in her hands,
tangling her fingers in his hair.

He planted a kiss in the triangle of coppery curls. "Just lie back and take it easy." Knowing exactly what she needed, he took her panties off the rest of the way.

"I don't think I can take it easy when... you're..." She moaned as he cupped her bottom in his hands and ran his lips down the inside of her thighs.

Kevin throbbed with wanting her, with the need to let go, too, even as she surrendered to him completely. She was so beautiful. So soft and feminine. Reveling in her responsiveness, he moved the pad of his thumb back and forth over the slick, sensitive spot. She closed her eyes, let her head fall back, her breathing soft and ragged. And still it wasn't enough. Needing to taste as well as touch, he loved her thoroughly with his mouth.

"I love it when you tremble for me," he said, enjoying how sexy and ravished she looked. How ready for him. "And open up for me like this." To their mutual enjoyment, he found her more wet and welcoming than before. Her thighs fell farther open; her toes curled. She rocked against him, close…so close.… "And come apart in my arms like this," he continued. "And let me know you're mine…."

Gasping, she clung to him. "I want you inside me, when I…"

Eager to please her, Kevin shifted upward. She closed her hands around his velvety hardness and guided him closer. He lifted her and touched her with the tip of his manhood in the most intimate way. Sensation built upon sensation and excitement roared through him.

"Yes," Noelle whispered, her response honest and uncompromising and unashamed. "Yes…"

Driven by the same frantic need, Kevin kissed her again, hotter, harder, deeper. He was determined to make this last, to make it real, to make it so amazing she would never want to be with anyone but him ever again. Fire pooled in his groin and then they were one. When she would have hurried the pace, he held back, making her understand what it was to feel such intense, burning need.

She wanted him, too. He could see it in her

eyes as she closed her body around his, taking him into her, giving him everything he had ever wanted, everything he had ever needed. Lips locked together in a fierce primal kiss, they moved together until what few boundaries still existed between them dissolved, until he was as deep inside her as he could go. Until they were lost in a completeness unlike anything Kevin had ever known.

Chapter Twelve

"What are you doing out of bed?" Kevin asked. It was 1:00 a.m. and, instead of cuddling next to him, Noelle was standing barefoot in his kitchen, washing baby dolls. She looked spectacular, wearing only her panties and one of his dress shirts. He felt her forehead and rubbed his thumb across her cheek. Thankfully, her fever seemed to have faded away. "I'll get up early in the morning and finish those."

Noelle flashed him a breezy smile that wasn't quite convincing. "You know the old saying—never put off until tomorrow morning what you can do tonight."

He noted the wariness in her eyes. Reminding himself that Noelle was an elusive woman, he framed her face with his hands. "Then I'll finish here," he told her softly, savoring the intimacy of the moment and the memory of the lovemaking that had happened earlier. "You go on back to bed."

He wanted to lie next to her, holding her close, breathing in the floral scent of her hair and skin.

"Not until the job is done," she stated stubbornly.

"Okay, then I'll help."

They worked in silence. "About us. This," she said eventually, teeth worrying her bottom lip. She looked at him with barely suppressed anxiety. "You know this is just a temporary fling."

He knew she wanted him to believe that. Why, exactly, he wasn't sure. Probing gently, he said, "You're just using me for sex, hmm?"

She flushed at his teasing tone. "What I'm saying is that given the chemistry between us, the time of year, this was bound to happen. But long-term, we may not be right for each other." She gulped. "And I didn't want you to think that I expected anything."

"Like a marriage proposal and a ring on your finger."

"Yes." She sighed in relief.

Kevin sensed she expected him to put up a fight, so she could list the reasons why they were all wrong for each other. Figuring it would take time to convince her the opposite was true, he changed the subject to his earlier meeting with Scooter Roth, bringing her up-to-date. "Apparently, he and his parents had a major disagreement about the course Scooter's defense was taking. Scooter ran off with only the clothes on his back and the cash in his pocket. The last couple of nights he's been sleeping in his car, trying to get up enough nerve to come forward with what he knew."

As she listened, Noelle's mouth fell open in shock. "Did law enforcement know he had run away?"

"No. His parents didn't report it. Which isn't surprising, given the fact that they were the masterminds of the identity theft ring, not him."

Noelle shook her head mutely. Her expression revealed little of what she was thinking. "How did they convince him to participate?"

Kevin knew Noelle had a big heart, but she was being too protective of a teenage boy she hardly knew. Especially given the fact that Scooter's actions had hurt Miss Sadie and countless others. "You don't think he volunteered to be a part of it?"

Outrage kindled in her eyes. "No."

Kevin wondered at her certainty. "Why not?"

Noelle shrugged. She shook her head and looked past Kevin, glowering at nothing in particular. "From what you and Miss Sadie said, he was a shy, nice kid." She leaned against the kitchen sink, arms folded in front of her, and took in a deep, steadying breath before returning her gaze deliberately to his. "So either Scooter was one heck of an actor—"

"Or con artist," Kevin interjected.

"Or he was facing enormous pressure from his parents to participate and take the fall, if and when they were caught, simply because he was a minor and would get off with a much lighter jail sentence than they would. Even so..." Noelle paused. "Scooter had to feel trepidation, going to the public library and using the computers there to send off criminal instructions that could—and eventually did—land him in jail."

"Scooter was scared. He felt he had no choice. His father had steered some of his clients in the popular investment firm he founded into highly risky but startlingly lucrative deals for years. Monthly returns had shown growth of up to thirty percent a year. The Roths and others were rich beyond their wildest dreams—at least on paper." Kevin took a breath. "When Mr. Roth finally realized the private placement group brokering the deals was nothing but a shell company and a vehicle for money laundering, he tried to get all of his clients' money out. The powers that be refused and fled the country."

"What happened next?" Noelle asked.

"Well, with clients wanting to remove money from the venture, Mr. Roth had to find the cash somewhere to reimburse them before they, too, discovered they had been bilked." Kevin explained. "Hence, the beginning of the identity theft. Mr. and Mrs. Roth already knew the wealthiest families in Houston. They used the information they had—about who would be out of town and when…and who could easily handle a fifty or hundred thousand dollar loss—to decide whom to target."

Noelle went back to scrubbing the last few dolls. "And Scooter was forced to play along."

Kevin nodded, picking up a towel. "He knew his parents weren't going to stop until they had paid back all Mr. Roth's clients and replenished the family bank account to a healthy twenty million. But once the operation became a huge success, he feared they weren't planning on closing up shop any time soon."

Noelle scrubbed at a stubborn stain on the forehead of one doll. "Why did it take Scooter so long to confess after he was arrested?"

Kevin handed her a scrubber sponge. "He was afraid if the truth came out his parents would go to jail and he'd end up in foster care."

Her brow furrowed. "I'd think the department would want him under police protection. At least until after he testifies."

Again, Kevin felt that jarring sensation that Noelle was a little too familiar with the way things worked in cases like these.

"I mean, I assume he's safe from his parents," Noelle continued hastily, "but from what you said, there are others involved who might not be so eager for Scooter to stick around and be able to testify about what he knows in court."

"True, which is why the feds have stepped in to assume custody of Scooter."

Noelle took the last doll out of the sack. "What about his parents?"

"They're already in federal custody, too." Kevin squeezed water out of one doll's hair, adjusting an arm that didn't seem to be on quite right. "Evidently they have some information on some pretty big fish."

"Poor Scooter. What a miserable Christmas."

"I know," Kevin agreed, moving some of the dolls to another counter to finish drying, "but he's still better off than he was." He'd had the feeling when he was talking to Scooter that his guilty secret had been crushing the teen.

Noelle let the soapy water out of the sink, her expression troubled.

"You really feel for him," Kevin noted.

She nodded, hanging up her dishrag and sponge. "Not that there's anything I can do for him," she sighed.

Kevin folded the empty sack and put it aside. "The district attorney's office understands Scooter was in way over his head. He'll be well looked after."

She shook her head in frustration. "Still..."

"What?" Kevin needed to understand.

She shrugged helplessly. "I'll never understand how parents can hurt their kids like that. Parents are supposed to love and protect their children with their very lives."

"The way you do Mikey."

"Yes. Even if you have to use a big plastic candy cane to do it," she joked.

They grinned, recalling the first day they'd met, and the complications that had ensued. Kevin knew she wanted him to drop the subject. He couldn't. Not when he was so close to discovering what haunted Noelle. Knowing they were talking about more than the Roth family, he used the opening given him and asked casually, "Were you hurt as a kid?"

"We all were—in one respect or another." She looked for one brief moment as if she wanted to take shelter in his arms and confess everything to him. Then her defenses returned and she said, as smoothly and evasively as ever, "But you know what I mean."

"The way Scooter Roth has been," he guessed, wishing he could make the sadness in her eyes go away.

"Yes." She turned her attention back to the task at hand. "So, do you have any more dolls in need of tender loving care?"

"Only one," Kevin replied mischievously. He picked Noelle up in his arms and carried her toward his bedroom. He joined her between the sheets and held her close. "And that—" he kissed her gently "—would be you."

"ARE YOU SURE you're up for this?" Kevin asked Noelle at suppertime the next evening.

As confident about the evening ahead as she

was about her growing closeness to the handsome detective, Noelle threaded a tiny snowflake earring through her lobe. "Social gatherings are my thing, remember?" Seeing she was having a little trouble, Kevin lifted her hair while she inserted the pin in its clasp. "Besides," she continued as he helped her with the other, "I've always wanted to learn how to make tamales."

He leaned against the bureau, while she simultaneously touched up her makeup in the mirror and kept a close eye on Mikey, busy playing with his cars and trucks on the floor. Kevin warned softly, "My whole family is going to be there."

So he had said—three times now. "Afraid they're going to give you a hard time about bringing me?"

Her gentle teasing provoked a sexy half smile. "Afraid they're going to give you the business?"

Should she be? Noelle wondered, checking out her reflection in the mirror from all angles. The slim-fitting, burgundy slacks and white turtleneck sweater looked good with her suede boots, but the outfit was still a little plain. She rummaged in her bag for the necklace that went with her earrings, and fastened it around her neck. Or tried to—Kevin had to help her with that, too. Noelle bent her head and lifted her hair from her nape. "I've already met all your brothers, your sister and one of your sisters-in-law." None had been anywhere near as distrustful as Kevin had initially been. And she had managed to pass muster with him!

Kevin's warm breath stirred the skin on her neck as he moved close enough to fasten the clasp. "But you haven't met my stepmother, Kate, and my dad and the rest of the family." Finished, he put his hands on her shoulders and turned her to face him. "And they can be awfully inquisitive when it comes to something interesting, like the new woman in my life."

Noelle was prepared for questions of that nature, even as she thrilled at the rough possessiveness in his low voice. "Is that what I am?" she teased, happier than he knew that he had thought to include her in the annual McCabe family festivity. She realized it meant he was getting as serious about her as she was about him. "Your woman?"

His mouth crooked again in that sexy grin. "What do you think?" He lowered his head and delivered a gentle kiss that quickly turned into more. Her lips parted beneath the pressure of his, and his tongue swept her mouth in long, sensuous strokes. His hands slipped around her and settled her more fully into his arms. Her breasts throbbed, her abdomen felt liquid and weightless, her knees weak. Lower still, where he pressed against her so intimately, she felt a tingling ache.

Then a tiny arm wrapped around her leg.

She and Kevin drew apart, grinning. "Hey there, buddy," he said.

Mikey held both his arms in the air. "Up!" he demanded. "Up."

Affection lighting up his handsome face, Kevin complied. He cuddled Mikey against his chest and looked at Noelle. "Ready?"

"As I'll ever be," she promised, going to retrieve their winter coats.

Kevin wasn't kidding, Noelle noted half an hour later. Their entrance into the steamy kitchen of Sam and Kate McCabe's large and comfortable Victorian home prompted a great deal of interest that continued well after Kevin made introductions and took Mikey off to play with the other cousins in the family room.

The wives were all there, cooking. Brad McCabe's wife, Laney. Riley's wife, Amanda. Kevin's newly married sister, Laurel, and Kate, his stepmother. Lexie McCabe, Lewis's new wife.

"What are your plans for Christmas?" Kate asked while whipping up a homemade enchilada sauce to flavor the filling.

"I'll be here—working—at Blackberry Hill." Noelle started helping Laney shred cooked pork for the tamales.

"What about your family?" Lexie asked, while combining masa harina, salt and baking powder. "Won't you miss them?"

"I lost my husband a few years ago, my parents when I was nineteen. So it's just Mikey and me."

"Miss Sadie—and her nephew, Dash Nelson—

are like family, though, aren't they?" Amanda asked, patting dry the corn husks that would be used to wrap the tamales for steaming.

"Yes. I've known them for about eight years now."

Will McCabe walked in as Kate was mixing the spicy meat filling. "This family is way too nosey," he teased, sending Noelle a sympathetic look.

Laurel frowned at her oldest brother. She folded open a shuck and spread two tablespoons of dough into a rectangle. "Maybe if you'd tell us something about your love life…"

"Nothing to tell," he stated flatly.

Kate shook her head at her stepson. She added meat filling down the center of the dough. "You see? That's the problem," she chided. "There should be plenty to tell about your love life, Will."

He turned to Noelle, more than ready to shift the attention to someone else again, while Kate rolled the sides of the tamale to seal the filling inside. "So…I gather you and Kevin are dating now?"

Noelle looked up and saw Kevin talking to his father in the backyard. Much as she wanted to acknowledge the truth, she didn't feel it was appropriate. Any information on their relationship should come from him. After all, this was his family. His news to tell, not hers. She smiled, shifting back into the familiar elusiveness that had served her so well over the years. "I think you'd have to ask him that," she said.

KEVIN KNEW HIS FATHER had something to say to him; he saw it in his eyes the moment he and Noelle walked in. It wasn't until they went out to get more wood for the fire that Sam spoke up. "Noelle Kringle is a lovely young woman."

Feeling a lecture about to commence, Kevin filled the canvas sling with neatly split oak logs. "Thanks. I think so, too."

Sam added kindling to the metal bucket. Worry permeated his low tone. "According to Miss Sadie, she's already spoken for."

Kevin stood slowly, dusting off his hands. "It's true. Dash Nelson plans to ask her to marry him."

Sam regarded him. "How do you know this?"

"Dash told me."

"And yet you're still going after her," Sam stated, clearly disapproving.

"She told me she doesn't feel that way about Dash. The chemistry just isn't there."

His father waited a beat. "And yet Dash Nelson is planning to propose?"

"Can't say I blame him."

Sam exhaled slowly. "Still…"

"I want her, Dad—in a way I've never wanted anyone else."

"That, I can see."

"You still have reservations," Kevin noted after a moment.

Sam rubbed his jaw, admitting ruefully, "I was in the middle of a love triangle once myself."

Kevin remembered. "With Kate and that guy she was engaged to before she married you."

Sam shot him a warning look, clearly trying to save him from a similar indiscretion. "It wasn't a pleasant experience, son."

Knowing nothing worth having ever came easily, Kevin shrugged. "It worked out for you, though."

"Because we were meant to be together," Sam pointed out calmly, no less ready to step in and protect Kevin now than he had been when his son was a child.

Kevin knew, even if his dad didn't, that that wasn't necessary. "Noelle and I are destined to be together, too," he stated firmly, pushing away any lingering worry he felt about the way she tended to withdraw into herself whenever he got too close or asked too many questions about her past. She might not have told him everything about her life yet. But she would. Kevin was sure of it. He just had to give her time.

Time and love.

"Sorry about the third-degree, but I figured we might as well get it over with," Kevin told Noelle later that evening, after they had returned to his place and put Mikey to bed.

Not sure when she had ever endured such relentless questioning, save for some of the job interviews she'd had, Noelle sent Kevin a wry look. She paused to take off one suede boot, then the other. "You knew your family was going to come on that strong, didn't you?"

"What can I say?" He turned off lights and locked up as they headed for the bedroom. "I haven't brought a woman to a family gathering in years."

Noelle took off her necklace and earrings and laid them on the dresser. "So someone mentioned."

He lounged against the bureau next to her, favored her with a sexy smile that did funny things to her insides. "I knew me showing up with you tonight would raise more than a few eyebrows."

Her heart pounded. "Why did you take me?"

His eyes locked with hers. "First, you're important to me, so it was important you be there with me tonight. Second, the McCabes are a forthright bunch and I know what a private person you are. I wanted you to know what you're getting into by getting involved with me."

"Is that what we're doing? Getting involved?"

Kevin gathered her in his arms, intuitively giving her the comfort and reassurance she needed. Hooking a thumb beneath her chin, he lifted her face to his. "This is more than a holiday fling, Noelle. What we've found with each other is the kind of relationship that lasts."

As if to prove it, he captured her lips with his in a kiss that was so unbearably sweet and tender it had her melting against him in abject surrender.

"We've only got one problem, that I can determine," Kevin murmured finally, lifting his head.

He regarded her in a way that left no doubt they would be making love very soon. "What's that?" she asked breathlessly.

He wrapped his arms around her waist. "The actual holiday. I signed up to work 10:00 a.m. to midnight both Christmas Eve and Christmas Day."

Noelle sighed and splayed her hands across his chest. "I'm working, too."

Regret darkened his eyes. "I wanted to have my Christmas with you and Mikey."

She lifted her shoulders in a shrug. "There's always the twenty-sixth. We could celebrate then."

He paused, his expression impatient. "How about the twenty-third and very early on the twenty-fourth, instead?"

"Tomorrow night is the Blue Santa party," Noelle pointed out.

"From four to seven. Cleanup will take less than an hour. We could come back here, put Mikey to bed, have our own merry little Christmas Eve a day early, and set it up so we could have our own 'Christmas morning' on the twenty-fourth before we both head off for work."

Noelle smiled, happiness bubbling up inside her. "You've really thought this out," she noted admiringly.

Kevin looked deep into her eyes. "I want to be with you."

It was that simple, and that complicated.

"I want to be with you, too," she whispered. More than she had ever thought possible.

Chapter Thirteen

"The children are going to be so delighted when they get these dolls." Miss Sadie beamed.

"They look like new," her friend Violet agreed.

Patsy dressed a colonial-era doll in a blue smock and white apron that had been washed, stitched and pressed to perfection. "And none of the dolls that were donated are currently available in the stores, so they'll be all the more special," she noted.

"You ladies have done a wonderful job," Noelle said, handing the quartet of Santa's helpers at Laramie Gardens Home for Seniors yet another group of baby dolls needing to be put back together. She put the gift-ready dolls in cardboard boxes brought in to transport them, then cast a glance at her son. Mikey was playing in a nearby corner of the activity room.

"Speaking of wonderful..." Marcia said slyly, looking Noelle up and down. "You've got quite a glow going in your cheeks."

Noelle flushed despite herself.

"Must be the brisk air outside," Patsy teased.

"Your eyes have been sparkling with excitement and happiness all morning," Marcia observed.

Noelle felt marvelous. It apparently showed. And why not, since she and Kevin had made hot, wonderful love before falling asleep the night before, and again just before dawn? Knowing there were other reasons for her happiness, too, she smiled. "I'm eager to go to the Blue Santa party this afternoon."

"We are, too," Violet exclaimed, handing over yet another perfectly attired doll.

Marcia worked a comb through another doll's hair. "I heard you were at Sam and Kate McCabe's last night for their annual tamale-making party."

Something else that had been done for a good cause. "And there are going to be plenty of tamales at the Blue Santa party this evening," Noelle said. "So be sure you ladies all get a taste when you go through the buffet line, because they are absolutely delicious."

"You've been seeing a lot of Deputy Detective Kevin McCabe," Patsy mentioned.

Seeing Noelle's surprised reaction, Violet shrugged. "It's all over town. Kevin hardly ever dates. So the fact he's so smitten with you....well, let's just say it's news."

Too much so. Noelle wasn't used to having her private life dissected for public consumption. She cast a look at Miss Sadie, wondering what her reaction would be.

The genteel old woman regarded Noelle with kindness. "You know, dear, I had always hoped that you and my nephew would someday tie the knot."

Patsy secured a cap on a doll's head. "Dash is handsome."

"And so successful and nice," Violet added.

Marcia nodded. "We all saw him on the news last night, talking about the trial he just won."

"Did he call you, dear?" Miss Sadie asked.

He had. Unfortunately, Noelle had had her cell phone turned off, and she hadn't checked her messages until this morning. "We've been playing phone tag. I know I'll see him at the Blue Santa party this afternoon. I'll congratulate him then."

"So you're dating him, too?" Marcia asked, obviously trying to make sense of Noelle's social life.

"Dash and I are friends," Noelle replied carefully.

"Very good friends," Miss Sadie corrected. "He's known Noelle for eight years now and has escorted her to many a social event."

"As a friend," Noelle repeated.

"Friendship is the start of many an enduring marriage," Miss Sadie countered.

"That's true," Marcia agreed. "My late husband and I started out that way."

Violet sighed, a wistful expression crossing her face. "Not me. With Hank and I, it was lust at first sight." She laughed, along with the other ladies.

Now that, Noelle thought, sounded like her and Kevin.

"I was first drawn to Sanford's big, lively

family," Patsy confessed. "They were such a loving, happy bunch."

Noelle couldn't help but admit she had loved being with the McCabes the evening before, feeling so welcome and included.

"I loved the security and kindness my Alfred provided," Miss Sadie stated. "Sort of like what Dash gives you, Noelle." She winked.

"Now, Sadie, stop matchmaking!" Marcia clucked.

"Can you blame me?" Miss Sadie looked at Noelle and defended her actions stalwartly. "I see how Dash lights up whenever he's around you and Mikey."

Noelle didn't want to hurt the older lady's feelings. "Mikey and I enjoy spending time with him, too."

Looking pleased, Miss Sadie continued pleading her case. "I know you and Dash started out as friends, Noelle, but you shouldn't let that discourage you from trying for something more."

"Miss Sadie!" she scolded.

"There's a closeness between you and Dash—

an emotional intimacy—that I never saw between you and Michael all the years you were married."

Kevin walked in and knelt to give Mikey a hug. It was clear from the carefully neutral expression on his face that he had overheard at least part of what had been said. To his credit, he acted as if he hadn't. "How's it coming, ladies?" He gazed at the hardworking quartet. "Are the dolls ready for transport to the center?"

"Five more minutes and they will be," Violet promised. "But you could start taking the ones in boxes out now."

Noelle stood. "If you ladies will keep an eye on Mikey for me, I'll give Deputy McCabe a hand."

"Go ahead, dear," Violet said.

"Mikey..." Noelle waited until her son turned and gave her his full attention. "Mommy is going to carry these out to the car. I'll be right back."

He bobbed his head up and down. "Okay." Then he went back to playing.

Noelle and Kevin headed out. "Seems like I interrupted something," he murmured as they left the building and stepped into the brisk December air.

"And not a moment too soon," Noelle declared. They crossed the parking lot, side by side.

He gave her a quick look as they reached his SUV. "Miss Sadie lobbying for a romance between you and Dash?"

"As always. Unfortunately, she also heard I've been seeing quite a lot of you."

"Yeah." Kevin nodded. "It's all over town."

Noelle noticed his look of smug male satisfaction. "I wonder how that happened," she said dryly.

He pulled his ear in mock thoughtfulness. "I might have mentioned it a time or two."

"And people might have noticed my car parked at your house all night the past two evenings," she mentioned. In Houston, it wouldn't have mattered. The people in her town home complex were too busy and preoccupied with their own lives to monitor the comings and goings of their neighbors. Here in Laramie, who was doting on whom was as newsworthy a topic as the results of the last election.

"There's a cure for that," he countered.

"Put both vehicles in the garage?" Noelle guessed.

He shook his head, looked deep into her eyes. "You could end all the speculation by marrying me," he said.

Noelle blinked, sure she hadn't heard right. She drew in a quick, bolstering breath, not sure from his expression whether this was his way of laughing off the gossip, or he was sincerely testing the waters. "Tell me that's not a proposal," she said casually, watching him shift his load to one arm and lift the rear door.

Kevin set the box of baby dolls inside the cargo area, then relieved her of the one she was carrying. "Well, I'm not exactly down on one knee," he drawled, turning to face her once again, "but the sentiment behind the statement is as real as the snow that will fall tonight."

Noelle looked at the wintry cloud cover overhead. She hadn't heard anything about snow in the forecast—the overnight low was slated to be thirty-four degrees. But Kevin had promised snow more than a week ago. Frustrated and confused, she focused on his handsome features once again. "What does that mean?"

"It means," Kevin explained with a calm, determined look that set her heart racing, "that if and when you decide you ever want to get married again, Dash Nelson isn't your only option."

"SO WHAT'S GOING ON with you?" Dash asked Noelle as the Blue Santa party got under way in the Laramie Community Center.

I am still reeling, Noelle thought, *from my quasi proposal from Kevin McCabe.*

Who knew what would have happened had they had the opportunity to continue their discussion? But Rio Vasquez had driven up and interrupted them just then. Dolls had to be transported. Noelle had to take Mikey back to Kevin's for a nap, prior to the event. And now that she was at the community center, with Mikey safely ensconced in the glass-walled nursery with the other toddlers at the party, she was too busy transferring baby dolls and brand-new tea sets into the pink gift sacks the female children were going to be taking home with them. Dash was pairing up the refurbished toy vehicles and new child-size tool benches with blue gift sacks.

She glanced through the doorway of "Santa's Workshop" to the center of the large party room, where Miss Sadie was sitting in her wheelchair, holding court. Flanking her were Violet, Patsy, Marcia and others from the seniors' residence. "What do you mean?" Noelle asked Dash.

"You didn't return my phone calls last night," he replied.

She flushed, guilty as charged. "I'm sorry. I didn't get your messages until this morning."

He positioned himself so Noelle had no choice but to look at him. "Anything I should know about?"

She wanted to tell him how she felt about Kevin. However, she knew now wasn't the time or the place.

"Look," Dash continued, frankly apologetic, "I know I've been busy with that trial…"

"I've been busy, too," Noelle admitted.

A strained silence fell between them. Years of emotional intimacy made it easy for Noelle to see Dash's hurt and bewilderment. He knew something fundamental had changed between them, but wasn't sure why. He frowned. "I heard you've been spending a lot of time with Kevin McCabe."

Noelle drew a bolstering breath. "He's a good man. I've come to...like him very much."

The glint of speculation in Dash's eyes was quickly replaced by regret. "How much have you told him?"

"Nothing yet," she admitted.

Dash studied her a long moment, before surmising unhappily, "But you're thinking about it."

Noelle nodded. She moved closer, her voice dropping confidentially. "I'm tired of hiding, Dash, of constantly having to withhold information and measure what I say." It was impossible to get really close to anyone—except Dash—the way things stood. She'd thought running from her past, pretending it had never happened, was the way to a secure and happy future for herself and her son. She saw now all it had done was put her in another prison, this one of her own making.

Dash studied her. "You feel you could trust him to keep your secret?"

It was certainly a leap of faith. But then that was what Christmas was all about. "Yes."

"But you're afraid."

Trust Dash to see the chinks in her armor and call her on them. Noelle's hands shook as she tied a ribbon on a gift bag. "He's a law enforcement officer." Who had already had his own professional reputation damaged once, by becoming involved with a woman who had a criminal past.

Dash returned to his chore, too. "McCabe might understand."

Noelle hoped he would. "But he might not." If he didn't, she knew their relationship would be over. She didn't want to risk it. Not this close to Christmas. Not when she had promised herself and Mikey a holiday full of love and happiness.

Dash clamped a steadying hand on her shoulder. "I did."

"I know that." Noelle let herself lean into his warm, fraternal touch. "And I appreciate it." Dash and Miss Sadie were still the closest thing to family she and Mikey had.

"But?"

Fear spread through her. "I'm not sure I want to ask Kevin—or anyone else—to do what you have done for me." Maybe Kevin never had to know. Maybe she could just let the hurtful part of her past finally be over.

Dash let her go, stepped back. "I've never minded keeping your confidence," he stated honestly.

"I know that." Noelle looked at him gratefully. "I also know it's not fair to saddle anyone else with the repercussions of my troubles. But maybe it's time I followed your initial advice to me and just came clean."

He looked at her sternly. "If you had done that years ago, it would be one thing. But you chose not to. There could be career repercussions. Even social ones. Miss Sadie will understand, of course. She has always loved you and Mikey, even without knowing the particulars of just how you and I came to know each other. But as far as other members of Houston society—I can't predict how they would react."

Not necessarily well, Noelle knew. She shrugged, asserting stubbornly, "If they hold my past against me, maybe they aren't worth knowing and doing business with, anyway."

Dash nodded, willing to leave the decision up to her, as usual. "Just know that I am here for you, always," he said.

Noelle knew that. The question was, would Kevin McCabe feel the same way, should the truth be told?

KEVIN WAS NEARLY to the administrative office to change clothes, when the cell phone at his waist began to vibrate. Recognizing the Houston number on the display panel, he picked up. "McCabe here."

"Hi, Kevin. It's Alicia Allen. It took some doing—I had to go back quite a number of years—but I finally got the information on Noelle Kringle you wanted."

Which meant, Kevin thought, that whatever it was Noelle was hiding had happened a long time ago. "I don't think I want to see it," he said.

The truth was, he already knew everything he needed to about Noelle. She was a kind, warm,

loving woman. A great mother. And a spectacular event planner. She still had trouble letting
people close to her, but he felt with time he could
change that. She'd already allowed him into her
heart and her bed. It wouldn't be long before
they'd be integral parts of one another's life. What
they had found was simply too good to give up
or sacrifice on the altar of any past mistakes.

"Too late," Alicia replied, efficient as ever. "It's
already on its way to you, air express. The
envelope will be delivered to your doorstep
sometime tomorrow."

Ah, well, he'd pitch it then. "What do I owe you?"

Alicia laughed. "A favor next time I need one."

"You got it." Kevin wished his friend a merry
Christmas and hung up. Anxious to get on with
the surprise he'd been promising, Kevin changed
into the red velvet costume and white beard, then
slipped out the back door of the community
center. Director-actor Beau Chamberlain, a legendary Laramie resident, stood waiting for him
in the vehicle-filled parking lot. Deputies had
already cordoned off the front. Two large

machines were placed on either side of the entrance, along with an old-fashioned sleigh with hidden wheels, drawn by a team of horses wearing fake reindeer antlers.

"You ready for some winter magic?" Beau asked.

When Kevin nodded, Beau gave the signal. "Snow" began pouring out of the sprinklers overhead.

"Wow," Mikey said, over and over, as he palmed the fat wet flakes falling out of the darkened night sky, courtesy of the local movie studio. He stuck his face in it, then reared back, grinning. "Snow," he said, amazed.

All the children at the party were enthralled by the surprise precipitation Kevin had arranged. Their parents were all grinning as Santa, aka Kevin McCabe, walked through the group, ho-ho-hoing and passing out presents to each of the kids. Noelle couldn't take her eyes off him. When a group of carolers approached and the sounds of music filled the air, the evening became even more perfect.

Half an hour later, when the precipitation finally stopped and "Santa" drove off in his sleigh, Noelle and Mikey went back inside to gather their belongings. Dash moved to her side. He regarded her confidently. "I'm going to take Miss Sadie to the nursing home, then I'll meet you at Blackberry Hill."

"Actually..." Noelle hesitated, sorry she hadn't made her plans clear to him sooner. "Mikey and I aren't going back to Blackberry Hill this evening. But we'll be there first thing tomorrow morning, to oversee the preparations for the surprise party tomorrow evening."

Disappointment gleamed in Dash's eyes. "I guess I don't have to ask where you'll be."

"You can reach me on my cell if you need me."

He clamped his lips together. "Look, I know it's none of my business," he began.

Noelle cuddled Mikey closer and looked at Dash over the top of his head. "Then maybe you shouldn't say it," she warned.

"I guess you're right." The presumption in Dash's voice faded. "Here and now isn't the place. But tomorrow night, before Miss Sadie and the other guests arrive for the party, you and I do need to talk about all that's at stake."

And the fact, Noelle added silently to herself, *that I have fallen head over heels in love with Kevin McCabe.*

"In the meantime, please, for all our sakes, don't get caught up in the festive mood of the holidays and do anything rash," Dash cautioned softly.

"Like want something reckless and wonderful for myself?" Noelle guessed at the direction the conversation was going.

"Exactly."

She sighed, her glance turning to the handsome detective striding toward her. It was too late for that. Way too late.

Chapter Fourteen

"Santa's coming tomorrow," Noelle told Mikey as she gave him a final kiss and hug and tucked him into bed.

"Santa," Mikey repeated happily, clutching his stuffed animals and blankets close.

"We'll see you in the morning," she promised.

"Sleep well, bucko," Kevin said.

Mikey grinned. He squeezed his eyes tight, made a wheezing sound meant to resemble snoring, then squinted up at them to see if they were watching. They laughed softly.

"Nighty-night," Kevin and Noelle said in unison.

"Ni'-night." Mikey grinned and snuggled down in earnest.

As they left the room, Kevin slid his arm around

Noelle's waist. She could smell the spicy after-shave he wore and the minty freshness of his breath. Her senses swam at his nearness, and what lay ahead. "Thanks for letting me be part of your Christmas," he told her softly.

Noelle turned and wrapped her arms around his neck, tipping her face up to his. The gentleness in his dark brown eyes mesmerized her. They exchanged smiles as a feeling of deep intimacy settled over them. "Thanks for going all-out to make it a holiday Mikey and I are both going to remember."

Flashing her a sexy smile, he ran his palm down her spine, then pulled her close. Feeling his arousal pressing against her, she trembled from head to toe. "You're talking about the snow, right?" His lips moved to the sensitive place behind her ear. He rained kisses down her neck and across her collarbone. Her breasts tingled as he slipped his fingers inside the V of her gray cashmere sweater and caressed her skin.

Just that quickly, Noelle felt herself begin to go weak. "And playing Santa, as well as including us in McCabe family festivities," she murmured as he kissed her again and again, then drew back to study her face. "I've always wondered what it would be like to be part of a big happy family at yuletide. Now I know."

"It can be pretty wonderful," he admitted with a satisfied smile.

Noelle took a couple of steps back. Safely out of reach, she pushed away the wave of longing she felt whenever he was near. "So wonderful," she confessed softly, "it almost feels like make-believe." She was terribly afraid she was letting the spirit of the season overtake her usual, practical view of the world. She had gone into this thinking—as did Kevin—they were adult enough, sophisticated enough, to be able to handle a short-term dalliance. Now, she knew she wanted more than a brief, passionate affair. He seemed to be indicating he was feeling the same. The question was, would his desire to be a permanent fixture of her and Mikey's life wane when the mistletoe and holly were put away? And he found out all she still had to tell him? Would he decide that getting involved with someone whose past was far from perfect was not what he wanted, after all?

"And yet," he said huskily, cupping a hand beneath her chin, "it is all too real."

Noelle curled into him even as a fresh wave of fear washed over her. "We've only known each other a couple of weeks."

He stroked a hand through her hair, reiterating gently, "Sometimes that's all it takes."

Noelle wished. Her emotions in turmoil, she ran a hand over his chest. "There is so much you and I don't know about each other." *So much guilt and shame. At least on my side...*

Kevin's gaze softened as he lifted her hand and brushed a light kiss across the knuckles. "So we'll find out," he promised.

Suddenly alarmed she was risking way too much way too fast, with a man who might not be able to accept her less-than-stellar past, she stated, "I have a child to consider and protect."

Some of the happiness faded from his eyes, replaced by a hurt that was just as deep as his joy had been. "You know I love Mikey, too."

Noelle flushed, aware she was doing it again— pushing away someone who cared about her, to keep her and her son from being hurt. "Yes. I do."

"Then what's this about?" he demanded.

She looked away.

He studied her silently, finally guessing, "You're annoyed I brought up the subject of marriage right before the Blue Santa party."

Noelle inhaled deeply, but retained her composure. That was certainly part of it, she acknowledged silently, letting her deep sense of self-preservation rescue her. She had hoped, if they ever talked about it, that it would be a much more romantic discussion than him simply telling her she had other options than a union with Dash.

She held up her hands, palms out. Deciding she needed to do something to prepare for the morning, she headed for the cache of gifts from "Santa." "I can't marry someone on impulse. Not again."

Kevin fell in step beside her, looking as if he wanted nothing more than to comfort her. "Is that what happened before?"

Still struggling to keep her emotions under

wraps, Noelle nodded. Together, they carried presents in from the master bedroom, where they had been hidden, and arranged them under the tree. Finished, she sank back on her heels, legs folded under her. "I'd only been dating Michael a couple of months when he suggested we go down to city hall." A more unromantic wedding couldn't have been had, but at the time she had been so desperate for some sense of security and stability, it never had occurred to her to hold out for more. Now, she saw that she had shortchanged them both by allowing passion and the promise of predictability to trump love.

Kevin dropped down beside her. He stretched out on his side. "You think that was a mistake?"

She turned her gaze from the glittering lights on the tree to his face. "In a lot of ways, yes."

"Such as?"

Trying not to notice how ruggedly handsome Kevin looked in the soft light, she shifted her weight so her legs were folded to the side. "Are you sure you really want to get into this?" she asked, tucking the smooth wool fabric of her long skirt around her.

He propped his head on his upraised hand. "How else am I ever going to understand you?"

And Noelle wanted that, more than she could say. Feeling she could confide in Kevin about this much, she drew a breath and began to talk frankly about her marriage. "Michael and I were never as close as I wanted to be. Part of that is my fault, I know. I've always had a hard time opening up to people."

"But not to Dash," Kevin swiftly pointed out.

So much for dating law enforcement, and or conversing privately with her old friend beneath the detective's nose. Aware Kevin was a little jealous and probably felt he had reason to be, Noelle swallowed. She traced the side seam of her skirt with her fingertip. "That's different."

Not about to let her off the hook that easily, Kevin trapped her roving fingers with his hand. "How?" he asked her bluntly.

Reluctantly, she forced her gaze back to his, letting him know with a look that he was the only one for her. She shrugged, aware she was parsing her words once again, unable to help it. She'd be darned if she would ruin the best holiday she'd had in years with the ugly truth. "Dash has known me for a long time," she allowed finally. *He knows the worst and doesn't care.* Just as she hoped Kevin someday would.

Kevin relaxed slightly. Their eyes meshed, held, even as he probed for an explanation. "How did the two of you meet?" he asked. "You never said."

She sighed. "Dash was my lawyer after my parents died. He helped me sort through the mess. And again after my husband died. And he pulled through for me when I wanted to start my own event-planning business."

Noelle could see Kevin was trying to make sense of the intimate way she had been talking with Dash earlier in the evening, at the Blue Santa party. "I guess his advice has always been solid." She forged ahead, revealing what she could.

Kevin pinned her with a look. "Fine legal advice doesn't usually equate closeness like that, Noelle."

"In our case it did. Maybe because I was so young—just nineteen when I first went to see him—and Dash was so helpful and kind. He understood how overwhelmed I felt back then. Whatever I needed, whenever I needed it, he was there."

"And yet you've never been romantically interested in him," Kevin continued.

"Like I told you before," Noelle said matter-of-factly, starting to feel more than a little irritated by his incessant need to figure it all out, "the chemistry just isn't there between Dash and me. Never has been, never will be. Not like it is with you and me." She decided she might as well tell Kevin at least this much. "The truth is, I've never felt passion like I do for you with anyone else."

"Is that what scares you?" he asked. A smile spread slowly across his face. "The ferocity of our attraction?"

Her breath caught in her chest. Unable to sit still, she moved over to rehang an ornament on one of the branches. Then she adjusted another. "And the fear that, if you really knew me, flaws and all, you wouldn't want to be with me anymore." And that hurt more than she could communicate.

"Hey." He sat up and caught her wrist before she could redecorate the whole tree. "I know everything I need to know about you," he told her tenderly. "I know you're loving and compassionate. Smart, witty, wise. Beautiful. Giving."

"Okay," she managed to reply, a little overwhelmed by both the feelings welling up inside of her and the nonstop compliments. "Those are the good qualities. Now for the bad…"

Kevin sobered and his fingers tightened on hers. "I know that deep down you're wary and cynical, like me. You're scared of loving the wrong person and getting hurt."

Noelle nodded, glad they were clear about this much. "Which is why I have trouble lowering my guard with you. Not," she added wryly, attempting to interject levity back into the conversation, "that this seems to scare you off."

He rubbed her lower lip with the pad of his thumb. "That's because I know that everybody's scared of something, scared to take that all-important first step."

Noelle knew what that first step should be. And as soon as this holiday was over…

"I have faith one day you'll trust in me as much

as I trust in you," he continued with the legendary McCabe confidence.

She shifted all the way into his embrace, laced her arms about his neck. "I think I'm already beginning to."

His head lowered. "And who said Christmas miracles don't exist?"

Their kiss was sweet and indulgent, and in Noelle's estimation, ended way too soon.

"Before we get carried away," Kevin told her, "I have something I want you to open." He handed her a flat square box wrapped in red foil.

"Good," Noelle quipped, bringing out her own gift from under the tree, which was half the size of his, "'cause I have a present for you, too."

They sat cross-legged on the floor, facing each other, so close their knees were touching. Kevin watched her intently. "You first," he said.

Hoping their gifts were as in sync as their emotions seemed to be, she opened it with fingers that trembled. "That's more than a key to my house," he teased, as she plucked the first item from the tissue paper, "it's also the key to my heart."

The second was a little harder to decipher.

"I know you live and work in Houston," he hurried to explain. "I know how much you value your independence. I still want to spend as much time as I can with you. So if this—" he pointed to the month-long work schedule in front of her "—doesn't mesh with your time off, then I want you to let me know so I can switch duty with someone else."

As the significance of what he had given her sank in, Noelle grinned, then began to laugh.

"What?" he asked, mystified.

She held up a hand. "Just open my gift to you," she advised.

With another look at her, Kevin did. Inside the gift box was a weekly engagement calendar sporting her own work information, and a house key to her place.

She chuckled as she linked fingers with him intimately. "Great minds think alike."

Kevin shifted her onto his lap, so her legs were wrapped around his waist. "People in love think alike..." he whispered, sifting his hands through her hair, over and over, until her heart was beating wildly out of control.

"Love or lust?" she asked, her insides fluttering.

Eyes lighting playfully, he lowered her to the floor. "Let's find out…." His mouth covered hers, demanding and receiving a response she hadn't known she could give, reaching a place inside her where no one had ever touched. She wanted to yield to him and the feelings that drove them both. Her emotions soaring, Noelle found comfort in being with him like this. She arced against him, her mouth hungry, her breasts pressed against the hardness of his chest. Lower still, a throbbing spread like fever deep inside her. Being with Kevin this way was beyond her wildest Christmas wish. It was her every dream fulfilled.

Kevin wanted this evening to be perfect for her. Forcing himself to ignore the urgent demands of his own body, he brought pillows and a thick throw into the living room. While she grinned, looking tousled and beautiful, he made a makeshift bed for them beside the blinking lights of the Christmas tree.

Her eyes locked with his, Noelle began unbuttoning her cardigan.

"Let me."

"It'll take forever," she protested.

"We have forever." Determined not to rush this, he relieved her of the sweater, the long-sleeved, white silk T-shirt underneath, the wispy lace of her bra. His body throbbed as he looked his fill. Sweet, sexy breasts and pouting pink nipples. She was so beautiful and delicate, with her copper hair a halo of tousled curls about her head, her lips damp and swollen from his kisses. Aware he'd never needed anyone this urgently, that he'd never had more reason to proceed with care, he stretched out beside her, then kissed her until they were both breathless with desire.

Her nipples budded against his palms as he caressed her breasts.

"Kevin," she moaned.

"You're not ready yet." He slid lower and sucked her nipples.

She moaned again, writhing. "Tell the rest of my body that."

He drank in the sweet feminine fragrance of her skin as he slid down her body, relieving her of skirt, tights, panties. He kissed her navel and the silky skin beneath. She moaned again as his hot breath ghosted over her skin, going lower yet, to silky thighs and the mound of copper curls. Loving the feel of her, he gently stroked her sensitive folds.

"Kevin," she pleaded again.

He tucked a finger into her soft core and found it damp, hot and tight, then touched her there with his lips. Still caressing her with his hands, he didn't stop until she was fiercely aroused and trembling. Her breasts were tight, aching peaks, and her legs fell open even more.

"Let yourself go," he whispered. She gripped his shoulders hard, arching up to meet him, heart thundering, breath rasping as she found the pleasure he sought to give her.

Kevin smiled contentedly. When her tremors subsided, he sat up and began undressing.

"Uh—no," she said, halting his hand with the pressure of her own. Her blue eyes sparkled. "I want to unwrap my present."

Kevin chuckled softly. He had known since he met her that he would never feel about another woman the way he felt about her. His eyes never leaving hers, he let her remove all his clothes. Then she cradled him with one hand, stroking him with the other.

"I'm not sure how long I'm going to last," he warned her gruffly.

She slid up to kiss him recklessly. "Like you said," she teased, "just let yourself go."

He moaned as she kissed her way downward once again, settling between his thighs. Her lips and hands moved over his skin, whatever shyness and reservations she'd once had, now gone. She seduced him like she couldn't get enough of him, her fiery hair spilling across his stomach like silk. Over and over she worked her tender magic until he shuddered uncontrollably. Knowing it would be over way too soon if they didn't switch gears, he caught her by the shoulders and shifted her so she was beneath him once again. His for the taking. "I want to be inside you."

Suddenly, he wasn't the only one shuddering with pent-up need.

"I want that, too," she whispered.

He was hard as a rock, throbbing, hot. Then he was inside her. Filling her. Creating an urgent need only he could satisfy. She wrapped her arms and legs around him, clasping him to her. Surrendering her heart and soul, just as he was giving his to her. Tightening her body around him, she took him deep, giving him everything he had ever wanted, everything he had ever needed.

Lips locked with hers in a fierce, primal kiss, Kevin pleasured her boldly. For the first time, he knew what it was to give—and take—without restraint. To love someone with every beat of his heart. To have his future defined.

"I love you," he whispered, knowing this was the best Christmas ever and that Noelle was his best gift.

She gripped him passionately as their desire skyrocketed them over the edge. "I love you, too."

AT 5:00 A.M., THEY HEARD Mikey stirring in his bed. Not sure who was more excited about the morning ahead, the little boy or the two of them, Kevin hugged Noelle and kissed the top of her head. "I'll start the coffee and turn the lights on."

Noelle pushed herself to a sitting position. Her curls were in riotous disarray after a night of passionate lovemaking. She looked deliciously tousled in her long-sleeved white T-shirt and velvety red pajama pants. She wrapped her arms around her upraised knees and watched with unabashed pleasure while he tugged on gray jersey sweats. "I'll change Mikey's diaper and meet you at the tree."

Kevin thought he was prepared for the joy of having Noelle and Mikey there to celebrate the holiday with him, even if it was a good twenty-four hours ahead of tradition. That was before he saw the ecstatic look on Mikey's little face when he toddled out and saw the gaily wrapped presents beneath the blinking lights of the Christmas tree. The innocence and wonder on the child's face reminded him of all that was good and right in the world. It made him want a family of his own. A family that included himself, Noelle and Mikey. And the look in Noelle's eyes, as her glance met his briefly over her son's head, said she wanted that, too.

"Look who was here," Noelle said softly.

"Santa Claus!" Mikey exclaimed blissfully. Not just once, but over and over, with every gift that was opened. They could barely get him to stop playing with his new trucks and cars long enough to eat breakfast. He was still happily ensconced in his loot when Kevin's sister, Laurel, stopped in to pick up Mikey and take him to the McCabes for the day.

"Thanks so much for doing this," Noelle said, handing over a diaper bag with all the essentials and another containing some of his new toys.

Laurel greeted Mikey warmly, then led the way back out to her sedan. "I'm glad to help." The two women waited while Kevin installed Mikey's car seat. "Besides, you'll have your hands full organizing the party out at Blackberry Hill."

Noelle shifted her son in her arms and kissed his cheek. "You're sure it's no problem to drop him off at suppertime?" she asked, while Mikey continued driving his toy car over her shoulder and down her arm.

Laurel smiled. "Not at all."

Noelle put Mikey in his car seat and buckled him in.

"See you later, bucko." Kevin leaned in to ruffle his hair affectionately.

Mikey merely grinned and continued driving his car across the padded side of his car seat.

Kevin stood with Noelle, waving, as Laurel drove off. He took Noelle's hand in his as they walked back toward the house. "I wish we had time to make love again." He wished they were already married, living together as husband and wife.

"How about tomorrow night?" Noelle asked, picking up the last of the wrapping paper. "After I've concluded all my work for Miss Sadie."

"It's a date." Kevin headed for his bedroom to change into his uniform.

Noelle began to pack her overnight bag. The doorbell rang and she went to answer it. An air-express courier stood on her front porch. "Package for Mr. Kevin McCabe."

"I'll sign for it," she said. She scribbled her signature, then took the thick, padded overnight envelope and walked back inside. She was about to set it down when she caught sight of the Houston, Texas detective agency in the return address. Okay, maybe this had nothing to do with her, she thought as she felt her knees begin to give way. Maybe he was working on a case.

Then why, her rational side argued as she sank weakly into a chair, didn't it go to the sheriff's department? Especially when he knew he was working today.

Was it possible, she wondered miserably, that Kevin had been checking up on her the entire time he was romancing her? Telling her he loved her while doing something like that behind the scenes?

He walked out in khaki pants, still shrugging on his uniform shirt. "Did I hear the doorbell?" he asked.

His gaze dropped to the package in her hand. She saw dread flicker in his eyes, and any doubts she had about his innocence fled. "You've been having me investigated," she said, bitterness welling up inside her. She'd thought her days of being accused and convicted without a trial in someone else's eyes were over. Apparently not. "I guess I shouldn't be surprised. You told me the first day we met that you did whatever necessary to uncover the truth and see every investigation through to the end."

He braced his hand on a bookcase. "Let me explain…"

She rose with regal grace and offered a tight smile. She hadn't been betrayed like this since she was eighteen. "That you snooped into my private life behind my back?"

His shoulders stiffened and his body took on defensive posture. "I knew something wasn't right."

Wasn't that an understatement and a half! She marched past him, hands knotted at her sides. "You're dead-on about that much."

He caught her arm and swung her around to face him. "I had cleared you of all involvement in the identity theft ring, but I couldn't shake the feeling you were hiding something."

She stared at him, aware that his gaze was a lot steadier than her heartbeat.

His voice took on a grimmer tone. "And that feeling intensified when you appeared to be lying to me about the basic facts of your background."

Her fury building at the knowledge he could have halted his investigation, but chose not to, she stared at the star-shaped badge on his chest. "How do you know that?"

Kevin dropped his hold and stepped back. He gave her a pointed look. "Public records state your father was an engineer, your mother a homemaker, that your family resided at one address in Houston until your parents' death when you were nineteen. None of that matched up with what you told me about your parents being involved in real estate appraisals and sales or moving every year or so."

Hurt beyond measure, she glared up at him. "So instead of asking me about the discrepancy, you hired a private detective!"

His eyes narrowed. "I knew I was too close to

the situation to identify and follow up on leads and make an honest assessment. I didn't want to make the same mistake I did with Portia."

Acutely aware of the differences between them, Noelle aimed an accusing finger his way. "But none of that kept you from sleeping with me or telling me you wanted to marry me one day."

He shoved a hand through his hair, looking more conflicted than ever. "I realized I love you."

That was the problem, Noelle acknowledged, her eyes stinging with unshed tears. She loved him, too. More than she had ever imagined she could love a man. "And what if what's inside this envelope makes you feel differently?" she demanded, her heart aching for all they had and now would just as surely lose. "What then? Am I just supposed to pick up the broken pieces and walk away?"

"Of course I don't want that," he told her gruffly, attempting to take her in his arms once again.

She held up a hand to stave him off. "But at least part of you would like to know that you haven't been imagining something nefarious going on."

To her disappointment, he couldn't completely deny it. "I make my living based on what my gut instinct tells me. You know that." He took a deep breath. "But, for the record, I was hoping what the detective agency found would clear you."

"But it didn't, did it?" Noelle asked, the old bitterness welling up inside her.

He studied her warily. "I don't know."

She folded her arms in front of her and regarded him skeptically. She was so hurt by what he had done she could barely breathe. "You're telling me the detective agency didn't call you when they hit pay dirt to tell you what they found? Before they sent the proof?"

A shadow of regret crossed his face. "They did."

"When?" Noelle demanded.

"Yesterday, when we were at the Blue Santa party," he told her plainly, his exasperation showing in the taut lines of his face. "I told them I didn't want to hear it."

"Right," she pointed out resentfully. "You wanted to spend one last night making whoopee before the mud hit the fan. So you asked them to express mail it to you instead."

She tossed the package at him.

He let it fall to the floor, made no effort to pick it up. The silence between them stretched out. Kevin's mask of civility fell away, and he looked as ticked off, frustrated and misunderstood as she felt. "For the record, I asked Alicia Allen, my friend at the detective agency, to call the search off yesterday morning. It was too late. The package was already en route. There was no way to stop it."

No way to un-ring a bell. Feeling her hopes for the future—their future—slip away, Noelle shifted her glance to the damning package. "You're right about that," she muttered, determined to keep herself from bursting into tears.

"I don't have to open the envelope," he told her.

She wished it were that simple. It wasn't. It didn't matter how much Kevin wanted to believe in her; he didn't trust her. Without trust, there could be no love. That, more than anything, was why she hadn't told him about her past. Because she hadn't wanted them to reach this juncture.

"You could live with that, Detective?" Wishing she was still naive enough to believe he could love her the way she needed to be loved, she searched his face. "Wouldn't not knowing what I've tried to hide from you eat you alive?"

He couldn't deny it.

Her heart breaking, she gathered up her things. "Rest easy, Kevin. No action on your part is going to be required—I have no outstanding arrest warrants on me…nothing that would require you to take me into custody. I also have no intention of making you the laughingstock of the department again." As he surely would be if word ever got out about her past….

"You're going to leave." He sounded every bit as devastated as she felt.

Exiting his life was the best thing she could do for him. And she loved him enough to make the sacrifice. "I have a job to do today," she told him numbly, aware she had never felt less like celebrating Christmas in her life. "As do you."

He moved to block her way. "Work can wait. We're more important."

A few hours ago she had thought so. That was before she had discovered his deception. "No, sadly, we're not. And that envelope," she choked out miserably, "proves it."

Chapter Fifteen

"It's for the best," Dash told Noelle several hours later when they met up at Blackberry Hill. "In your heart, you know that."

Did she? Noelle wondered disconsolately as they brought in trays of prepared food for the open house. The last few weeks had been the most emotionally fulfilling of her entire life. She had been ready—and willing—to tell the sexy detective everything and build a life with him. Only to discover Kevin McCabe was every bit as capable of lying and cleverly misleading her as her parents had been. They had used her to further their greed, then abandoned her at the first sign of trouble. Kevin had pretended to accept her, flaws and all, while secretly furthering the investigation he knew would give him reason to end their tryst. The cruelty of his deception cut deep, obliterating the first real Christmas spirit she'd had in years. As much as she loved Miss Sadie and wanted the holiday party Dash was throwing for his beloved aunt to be a success, Noelle wasn't sure she could get through the event. At least not with her professional cheerful demeanor intact.

"I understand passion, Noelle," Dash continued earnestly. They went back outside to her van. "Heaven knows I've had my fair share of flings. But when it comes to settling down and taking on a lifetime partner—a father for your son—you've got to look for more than just an accelerated heartbeat and the excitement that being with someone so different from us brings."

Noelle carried the bakery goods, while Dash toted the staples for the bar. "You and I aren't the same, Dash. I didn't have a privileged upbringing."

"You'd never know it by looking at you now." His gaze swept over her. "You're an incredibly sophisticated woman."

Noelle guessed at the nature of Dash's thoughts. "Too sophisticated for this one-horse town?"

He helped her out of her coat, then shed his. "You're a city girl. Always have been, always will be."

"Not by choice," Noelle corrected, striding over to the sink to wash her hands. Her parents had needed the anonymity of a large population to hide in. Eventually, Noelle had needed the same to preserve her secrets. Later, when she had married, Michael's work had necessitated they live in Houston. When her husband died, Noelle had stayed because that was where her business was. She'd never even looked at the possibility of residing in a small town, until the past couple of weeks. The truth was she'd loved spending time in Laramie almost as much as being with Kevin. For all the good it had done her, she reflected sadly, now that her shame had caught up with her once again.

Dash brought in the china serving platters from the dining room. "You have to put what happened with your parents behind you."

Noelle artfully arranged slices of fruit and cheeses on a tray. "I've been trying to do that."

He began setting up the bar. "And you've succeeded."

She fit specialty breads into cloth-lined baskets. "Really? Then why did my past just rear its ugly head?"

Dash stopped what he was doing and clasped both hands on her shoulders, forcing her eyes up to his. "Because you put your hope and faith in the wrong person," he told her. "I'm the one you should trust, Noelle. I'm the one who will make you happy."

The old look was back in his eyes. The look he'd had when they first met, when he'd thought that maybe the two of them should start dating. Wishing she could forget her romantic notions about what love should be, and just appreciate what was between her and her trusted friend, Noelle offered a hesitant smile. She knew Dash would do anything for her and Mikey, including rescue them from the mess she had made of things with Kevin McCabe. If only she had pledged her heart to someone like Dash, who would allow her to keep her guard up, instead of someone like Kevin, who had demanded she open herself up to him, heart and soul.

"I'm the one you should have been turning to the last few weeks, Noelle," he said, reprimanding her softly.

Noelle saw the mixture of jealousy and determination in Dash's eyes. Knew he deserved better than she could ever give. Yet he would undoubtedly settle for so much less, if only she would agree to turn their relationship from friendship into something more.

So why couldn't she do it? Something was stopping her—but the question was *what*. Foolish dreams of a man who was now out of her reach?

Dash returned to his usual matter-of-factness. He regarded her fondly, all capable attorney once again. "We'll talk about this later, at the appropriate time. Right now, I'd better go over to Laramie Gardens and pick up Aunt Sadie."

Noelle glanced at the clock. Dash was right. The completion of this far-too-complicated discussion could wait. Guests would start arriving in the next ten or fifteen minutes. She still had a lot to do to finish setting up.

The next few hours passed rapidly. Blackberry Hill was filled with old friends—and new—by the time Miss Sadie arrived in her wheelchair. Dash poured drinks for everyone. Noelle answered the door, made sure the buffet was continually replenished with holiday goodies, and paid special attention to the guest of honor.

She had just emerged from the kitchen, with another cup of cinnamon tea for Miss Sadie, when Dash's aunt motioned her closer. Sadie accepted the steaming beverage, then gestured for Noelle to back up just a little. "Not too far…" she cautioned mysteriously. "Yes, right there."

Figuring it was some sort of Christmas surprise—maybe a toast in her honor for the success of the gathering?—Noelle complied. Dash stepped in close beside her. Too late, Noelle realized they were directly beneath the mistletoe.

"The floor is all yours," Miss Sadie told her nephew triumphantly.

Noelle turned to her old friend.

Dash stood before her, a small blue velvet box in his hand.

The room grew hushed.

Oh, no...Noelle thought.

It was too late.

He flipped open the lid of the box and revealed a sparkling diamond ring inside. "Noelle Kringle," he said, going down on one knee. His eyes locked with hers. "Would you do me the honor of marrying me?"

"THERE YOU ARE!" Laurel said breathlessly. It was 11:00 p.m. on Christmas Eve and all the businesses in town were closed. The only people who seemed to be out were those attending midnight church services.

Laurel folded her arms in front of her, shivering in the cold, wintry air, as Kevin finished feeding coins into the vending machine outside the supermarket. "You were supposed to drop by Mom and Dad's on your dinner break."

Kevin popped the tab on his can after retrieving a soda. "I was busy."

"You were avoiding."

Having his family ask questions about Noelle and Mikey? You bet he was. Kevin took a long drink of soda. He shot his happily married baby sister a disparaging glance meant to chase her away. "Like you'd know anything about my life."

Laurel arched her brow in typical know-it-all fashion. "I'm aware Noelle just got a marriage proposal from someone else a couple of hours ago."

Kevin felt a stab to the gut that had nothing to do with the amount of caffeine he had ingested on an empty stomach. With effort, he kept his demeanor supercool. "Yeah? How do you know that?"

Worry lit Laurel's gentle eyes. "Because I happened to be at Blackberry Hill, dropping off Mikey, shortly after the big event."

Which meant Dash Nelson had gone through with his plan to propose to Noelle in a room full of people. Kevin quaffed the rest of the drink. Aware that all the beverage had done was make him colder, he crumpled the empty can in his fist. "I gather she said yes?"

Laurel leaned against the storefront. "She didn't say no."

Briefly, hope flared, then was quickly snuffed out. Kevin stared at the streetlamps shining overhead. "Not saying no is the same as saying yes."

As usual, Laurel was slow to give in. "Not necessarily."

And he'd thought he had a tough time with Rio Vasquez earlier. "Why do you think this matters to me?" Kevin strode toward his squad car.

Laurel bounded ahead, to keep him from opening the door to the driver side. "Because she's in love with you and you're in love with her."

Kevin felt a stinging in his eyes that had nothing to do with the cold wind cutting through his clothing. "Not anymore."

Laurel tipped her chin up stubbornly. "I know you care about her more than you've ever cared about any woman in your entire life."

Kevin scowled. "I don't remember telling you that."

She shrugged. "You didn't have to say a word. It was written on your face every time you looked at her." She stepped nearer, a pesky little sister at her worst. "You. Love. Her, Kevin McCabe."

Kevin mimicked her emphatic tone. "It. Doesn't. Matter."

Laurel blew out a gust of air, looking as if she wanted to throttle him. "What happened? You have to talk to someone. It might as well be me."

She had a point there, Kevin realized. He leaned against the squad car. "Noelle found out I investigated her."

"So?" Laurel looked confused. "That's your job."

If only he had contained his curiosity to that. "I hired someone to go deeper than I could go as a member of the sheriff's department," he admitted reluctantly.

"Why?"

"Because I felt she was hiding something."

"And?"

"Obviously, my gut was right," Kevin retorted without an ounce of satisfaction. "She was."

"There's no way I'm going to believe she's a criminal."

Kevin looked up at the night sky, wondering when the best holiday he'd ever experienced had turned into the lousiest. The silence deepened.

"What exactly did the private investigator find out?" Laurel asked eventually.

"I don't know." Kevin stared at the manger scene in front of the church. "I haven't read the file."

Laurel shook her head as if that would clear it. "Why not, if you're broken up?"

Kevin cleared his throat. That was hard to explain. He was still curious, but he no longer needed to know every little thing about Noelle and her past. Maybe because through his love he had also found faith. Noelle was a kind, trustworthy person. Good through and through. He knew that as certainly as he was standing here. He was just sorry it had taken him so long to open up his heart again.

Laurel studied him. "It's because you still love her," she said triumphantly.

No denying that, either. For all the good it was going to do him.

"You still have a chance to make this right," she insisted.

Kevin thought about the look on Noelle's face when she'd found that express mail package and realized the depth of his betrayal. "I don't see how," he said gruffly.

Laurel gave him an encouraging pat on the arm. "It's Christmas. Think about that. And go from there."

NOELLE STARED AT THE clerk behind the desk at the Laramie Inn with a sinking feeling of dread. "You don't have any rooms?"

"I'm sorry," Red Marberry, the owner, repeated kindly. "It's Christmas Eve. We're totally booked and so is the other motor lodge in town. A lot of people visiting family here need a place to stay."

"I guess I should have thought of that." Noelle cradled the slumbering Mikey against her shoulder. She should have done what Miss Sadie and Dash suggested and bunked at Blackberry

Hill, as planned, for the next two nights. Instead, she had impulsively gone out into the cold winter evening. Only to lose her nerve and end up here instead.

Red Marberry stroked the white handlebar mustache and soft fluffy beard that made him look like the real Santa. "Look, I'll call around," he told her sincerely. "I'll find something…even if the wife and I put you up ourselves."

Noelle appreciated the kind offer, but she couldn't impose on two strangers on this most important holiday, no matter how generous they appeared. "That won't be necessary," she said, as a door opened and closed behind her on a cold gust of air. "I can always go back to Blackberry Hill."

"That won't be necessary, either." A familiar voice sounded in her ear.

Noelle turned to see Kevin McCabe standing there in a long brown duster and full tan uniform. His hat was tugged low across his brow. His cheeks and nose were red from the cold, his eyes alight with curiosity and another emotion she couldn't quite identify.

"I'll handle this," Kevin said, smiling down at the angelic looking Mikey and draping a light but ever so protective hand on her shoulder.

"That okay with you?" Red Marberry asked.

Noelle nodded, joy filling her heart. Suddenly, it seemed like Christmas again. And a potentially merry one at that. Maybe her first instinct tonight hadn't been so far off, after all. There was only one way to find out. Heart pounding, Noelle walked out with Kevin toward the van she'd left parked beneath the portico.

He stood to block the wind. As he offered a sexy smile, the cleft in his chin deepened. "So, no room at the inn, hmm?"

Noelle reached into her pocket and handed over her car keys. "Appears that way."

Kevin hit the unlock button on the keypad twice. He slid open the rear passenger door. "Want to come home with me?"

She had been wishing he would ask. She looked up at him, hoping this meant what she thought it might. "You're off duty?" Her voice sounded rusty, even to her own ears.

"As of five minutes ago," he told her soberly, "yes."

Noelle put Mikey back in his car seat. Kevin got in his patrol car and followed her the short distance to his home. He carried the sleeping child inside while Noelle quickly set up Mikey's pack-and-play crib in the spare room. Tired out by the holiday activities, her son barely stirred as she arranged his blanket and stuffed animals and settled him in.

For a moment, Noelle and Kevin stood there side by side, watching Mikey sleep. Satisfied he was set for the night, Noelle slipped soundlessly out of the room. Kevin followed. As soon as they were out of earshot, his glance slid to her left ring finger.

"You heard about the proposal and how I politely ducked having to reply at the time," Noelle guessed.

The way he was looking at her made her heart speed up. "I gather from the fact you left Blackberry Hill that your answer—"

"Was a gentle but firm no," Noelle confirmed.

Pleasure lighting his eyes, he tucked a curl behind her ear. "Any particular reason?"

Noelle reached over and slipped her hand into his. "I don't love Dash in that way. I love him as a brother, friend and family member. I think he and Miss Sadie finally understand that now."

Kevin's glance turned even more possessive. The hand on hers tightened even as he slid the other around her waist and tugged her nearer still. "They didn't kick you out, did they?"

"Oh, no." Noelle cuddled against his warm body, feeling she had come home again, at long last. "They wanted me to stay the night, particularly in light of the sit-down Christmas dinner I'm supervising there tomorrow."

"But you chose to flee instead."

Noelle decided to surrender her pride completely and tell Kevin what was on her mind. "I wanted to talk to you. The sooner, the better. Then I started thinking how presumptuous it would be for me to land on your doorstep in the middle of the night, on Christmas Eve, no less, given the way things ended this morning."

He nodded. "You did storm out on me."

Noelle flushed. "And you let me."

"My mistake." He ran a hand up her spine, eliciting tingles of desire. "Which was why I was coming to find you when I saw your minivan at the inn."

"Why?" she asked tentatively.

His expression was earnest. "To tell you not to marry Dash Nelson, to marry me."

The words she had been waiting for warmed her heart. "Even knowing all that you know about my past?" she asked tremulously, feeling her eyes mist up.

He shrugged and glanced toward the coffee table. Noelle noticed the express mail envelope there. It remained just as she had seen it this morning—unopened. "Why didn't you read what was inside?" she demanded nervously. Surely he had been curious!

He shrugged. "Because I figured if there was anything I should know, you would tell me."

Just like that, she felt as if a huge weight had been lifted off her shoulders. "And if I choose to tell you nothing?" she asked, needing to be sure.

To her relief, Kevin gazed straight into her eyes.

"Then it's a closed case," he told her soberly. "I'll never know. And we'll never bring it up again."

Realizing his love truly was without conditions, she stared up at him in wonder. "You would do that for me?" she whispered, tears blurring her vision.

Kevin nodded. "I would do anything for you," he said gruffly.

"That is one huge sacrifice on your part."

Not so much, Kevin thought, given what he was receiving in return. "Haven't you heard?" He bent his head and kissed her, his heart full of love for the woman in his arms. "Giving is what Christmas is all about."

She returned his caress, then slowly drew away. Taking him by the hand, she led him over to the sofa. "I need to give you something, too—the truth."

She turned to face him, her bent knee nudging his thigh. "My parents were part of a small group of con artists who committed mortgage fraud, long before it became popular. My mother was the sales agent who produced phony buyers to purchase properties from banks, and my father appraised the homes for more than they were worth. Another partner was a mortgage expert who brokered loans from legitimate banks, and the fourth swindler was an attorney who did all the legal work." Her eyes glittered with pain while she regretfully recounted the truth. "The four of them went from boom area to boom area. That's why I moved so much as a kid."

"Because your parents were trying to stay a step ahead of the law."

"Right. Anyway…" Noelle drew a quavering breath. She captured his hand with her own. "I knew nothing about it until I was almost eighteen, when the FBI hauled me in for questioning. Apparently, my parents had been using my name and social security number on some of the paperwork. Aware they were close to getting busted, my parents gave me a crash course on thievery so it would appear I knew what I was talking about, and asked me to take the fall."

Suddenly, it all made sense. "Just like Scooter Roth's parents did him." No wonder she had gotten so upset about the poor kid's plight!

Noelle's eyes turned even grimmer. "I couldn't do it, though. Not even for five minutes. Anyway, I began helping the FBI by providing information on my parents' partners-in-crime. Threats were made. I was put in the witness protection program."

Needing to hold her, Kevin shifted Noelle onto his lap. "What about your parents?"

Sadness clouded her eyes. "They went on the lam the minute they realized I wouldn't play along."

Kevin was stunned by the cruelty. "They just left you behind?"

Noelle nodded glumly. "Without a lawyer. Without any money or anyone to stand by me." She laid a hand on his chest. "I was so scared."

"And that's where Dash Nelson came in," Kevin guessed, covering her hand with his own.

Noelle nodded. "Dash was just out of law school, and he was assigned by the court to represent me. He made sure my rights were protected, even as I cooperated with authorities. He was there again when my parents' and their business partners' private jet went down, killing everyone on board. Suddenly, I was not in jeopardy anymore, but my real name was still mud, so I had the option to go with the identity the FBI had provided for me, Noelle Smith…or go back to my real name."

"So they gave you the name Noelle."

"They gave me the name Smith. I chose Noelle. I thought it would symbolize a new beginning and a purity of spirit. Of course, at that point," she added wryly, "I had no idea I would later meet and marry a man named Michael Kringle…but that's another story."

One that Kevin had to hear. "Did he know?"

"No." Noelle's expression grew conflicted once again. "At first I was afraid to tell him. Then I didn't want to burden him. And then it became this lie between us, and I didn't know how to get around it, how to let him close." She took a deep breath. "I didn't want the same thing to happen between you and me."

"But I was investigating you, in connection with another fraud and embezzlement charge."

"Obviously, I didn't want to bring it up for fear it would put me at the top of the suspect list. So

I kept silent, even though I could see you knew I was hiding something."

"And you continued to keep your past a secret from everyone."

"I had seen how people who knew my family looked at me when the truth about what my folks had done originally came out. I didn't want to go back to that. Because my photo had been kept out of the papers, no one knew what I looked like. So it was easy enough to go with the new life history and name the FBI gave me. If I had told the catering company I worked for that I had a criminal past, I never would have been hired. Same now, as an event planner. So I just tried to view the new beginning as a rebirth, and a chance for a fresh start, sans the baggage of my parents' crimes."

Kevin brushed a strand of hair from her cheek. "And that worked until I came along," he surmised.

"I would like to say that is true. It's not. I've struggled with all the lies required of me for a long time. It's been really hard. My fear of messing up is why I haven't been able to let people close."

"Does Miss Sadie know?"

"Only Dash. And of course, the FBI, but I no longer have any contact with them. And now you and the P.I. you hired."

Kevin held her tenderly. "I'm sorry about that."

Noelle shifted more comfortably on his lap. "I'm not." She draped her arms around his neck, gazing into his eyes. "This whole thing made me realize I need to be free. I need to stop lying about every aspect of my previous life and tell the truth. Even if it means people don't want to associate with me anymore."

Kevin was glad she had decided to cut herself free of the chains of her past. The decision made their very first Christmas together all the more special. "No one who knows you is going to blame you." He smoothed a hand through her hair.

She regarded him, soberly. "What about you?"

"I think you're a remarkable woman," he told her, kissing her with all the love and passion he possessed, letting her know he would stand with her forever. However, knowing that there were still some very important things to be settled, he reluctantly ended the caress. "And I'm incredibly lucky to have met you and Mikey and have you in my life. Only two questions remain. The first is can you forgive me?"

Happiness gleamed in her eyes. "The answer to that is yes," she answered with a smile that said she was set to embrace their future with Texas-size gusto. "And the second question?"

Kevin grinned. "Just what is it going to take to get you to move here to Laramie and be my wife?"

Epilogue

Six months later...

The warm June evening was scented with flowers. A string quartet played in the church sanctuary, while guests filtered in for the most anticipated nuptials of the season.

Only one thing was wrong with this picture....

Noelle propped both hands on her hips. She looked at Kevin sternly. "You are not supposed to be in here."

Even though, she admitted, she had been half hoping he would somehow get past the female sentry standing guard, and sneak in to see her.

Handsome as ever in an elegant black suit, crisp white shirt and striped tie, he sauntered nearer with customary self-assurance. One hand tucked behind him, he winked at her. "I won't tell if you won't."

Oh, dear. The bad boy in him got her every time.

Noelle melted into the warmth of his one-armed embrace. She tipped her head up for a brief, possessive kiss, then drew away. "What do you have behind your back?"

Slowly, he released her and brought his hand around. Noelle laughed when she saw the plastic candy cane. "Think we can work this into our wedding ceremony?" he quipped.

"Not likely," she teased back, "since the evening does not have a Christmas theme."

"Aw, shucks!" Kevin flashed her his best rueful grin. His gaze roved her ivory silk faille suit. "I guess we'll have to save it for later."

Later? She watched him lay it across a nearby folding chair. "What are you planning to do with it?" she asked, curious as ever.

"I don't know." He pretended to study the lawn ornament that had helped bring them together. He returned to her side, delivered another deep, searching kiss that stirred her heart. "I thought we'd take it on our honeymoon."

Noelle laughed softly. Her pulse raced with anticipation. "You're funny," she countered dryly. No way were they checking into the Ritz-Carlton with that.

"Seriously, we owe that Christmas lawn ornament a lot." He regarded it with exaggerated solemnity. "You might say it brought us together."

"Something did," she agreed, lacing her arms around his neck. They shared another long, soulful kiss that soon had her aching for more.

Kevin smiled down at her in a way that let her know just how connected they had become. "I want you to know that you've made me happier than I have ever been in my entire life."

"I am, too," Noelle murmured. With Kevin by her side, she had found the strength to make public the truth about her tarnished past. Her honesty had cost her many a client in the upper echelons of Houston society, a fact that had made it easier for Noelle to move her event-planning business to Laramie County. She no longer had dozens of black tie events to supervise. The parties she organized now were smaller, more intimate, and in many cases, much more meaningful. Her satisfaction in her work had never been greater.

Mikey was happy, too. He loved his new preschool. When she had to work in the evenings, Kevin—or another McCabe—was always available to care for the little boy. Dash and Miss Sadie still saw him frequently, too. Mikey had never had so much love and attention. He was thriving.

The door to the anteroom opened. Dash walked in, his aunt on his arm. Having made peace with the fact that Noelle and he were destined for a close friendship and nothing more, Dash was now dating a Houston attorney who worked for a rival law firm. They were getting rather serious, it seemed.

"We have something to give you," Miss Sadie announced cheerfully.

Her hand trembling only slightly, the elegant older woman pressed a dainty lace handkerchief into Noelle's hand. "I carried this when I married Alfred. I like to think it brought me sixty-two years of happily wedded bliss. I hope it brings you luck, too."

Noelle hugged her dear friend. "Thank you, Miss Sadie."

Dash shook hands with Kevin. The men exchanged warm, sincere looks, indicative of the deep and enduring friendship they'd formed over the last six months. "You're a lucky man," the attorney said. "But then you know that."

Kevin smiled. "Yes. I do."

Dash turned to Noelle, hugging her. "Appreciate this guy," he instructed. "He's one in a million."

"That I know." She smiled, glad she had the support and blessing of her two old friends.

Dash offered his aunt his arm again. "We'd better get you seated."

"Yes, dear." Sadie patted Dash's arm. "We don't want to keep your date waiting. She is such a lovely young woman…."

"She is," Noelle and Kevin agreed.

No sooner had Dash and Miss Sadie left than the door opened again and Mikey galloped in with Kevin's sister. Laurel looked resplendent in her matron of honor finery. "Mommy!" Mikey announced proudly, holding the child-size velvet cushion aloft, "I got a pillow! With rings! See?"

Noelle nodded solemnly. "Yes. You do." Fortunately, the rings were attached with slender but sturdy Velcro fasteners that would keep them from getting lost during Mikey's much-rehearsed trek up the aisle.

Laurel smiled and cleared her throat delicately. "Reverend Bleeker wanted me to tell you the bridal party is lining up. Not that he would approve of you being in here, Kevin." She glared at her brother.

Kevin chuckled, not the least bit repentant, then leaned over to give his bride another kiss. "I guess I'll see you out there?"

Noelle nodded and picked up her bouquet.

Moments later, she was following her son down the aisle, knowing she had never been happier. Her heart soared as vows were said, rings exchanged, permission to kiss granted. And she could tell by the look in Kevin's eyes that he felt the same.

As his head lowered to hers, she whispered, "I love you, Kevin McCabe."

He smiled. "I love you, too, Noelle McCabe." Then he kissed her, ending the ceremony and sealing their fate.

From the front pew, Mikey—unable to contain himself a moment longer—let out an exuberant cheer and raced up to join them.

Other voices followed and it felt like the best Christmas ever all over again.

Their new life together had begun.

* * * * *